P9-CAN-341

Childcraft

FOLK AND FAIRY TALES

MILO WINTER

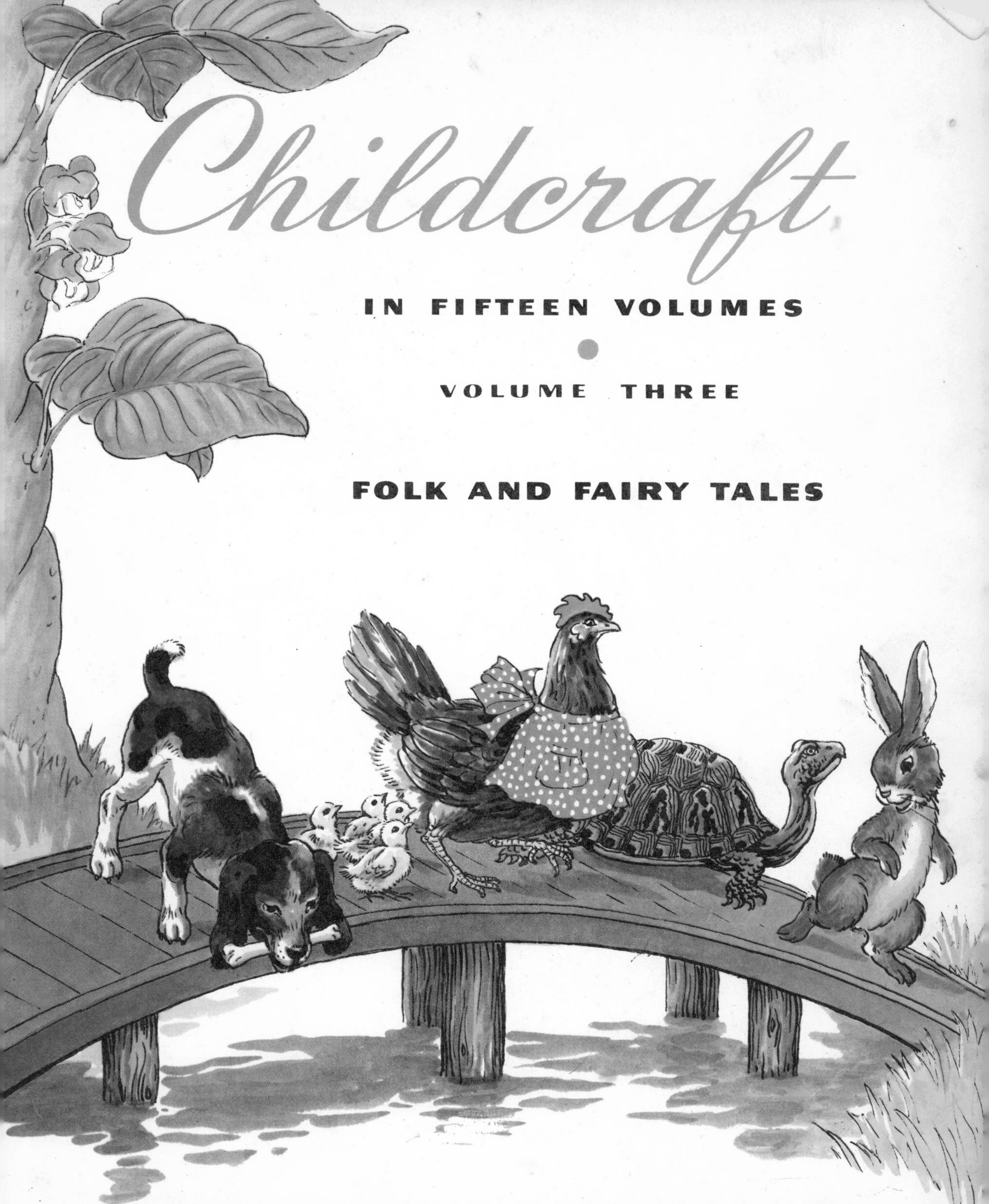

Childcraft

IN FIFTEEN VOLUMES

•

VOLUME THREE

FOLK AND FAIRY TALES

FIELD ENTERPRISES EDUCATIONAL CORPORATION
Merchandise Mart Plaza · Chicago 54, Illinois

1961 Edition

CHILDCRAFT
(Reg. U.S. Pat. Off.)

Printed in the United States of America

FAA

CONTENTS

FAVORITE NURSERY STORIES

FOLK AND FAIRY TALES

AESOP'S FABLES

ACKNOWLEDGMENTS

The publishers of CHILDCRAFT gratefully acknowledge the courtesy of the following publishers and authors for permission to use copyrighted stories, poems, and illustrations:

D. Appleton-Century Company: "Prince Wicked and the Grateful Animals" from *More Jataka Tales* by Ellen C. Babbitt, copyright 1922 by the Century Company.

Coward-McCann, Inc.: "Gone Is Gone" by Wanda Gág, copyright 1935 by Wanda Gág; "Hansel and Gretel" from *Tales from Grimm*, freely translated and illustrated by Wanda Gág, copyright 1936 by Wanda Gág.

Harcourt, Brace & Company, Inc.: "The Steadfast Tin Soldier" from *It's Perfectly True and Other Stories* by Hans Christian Andersen, translated by Paul Leyssac, copyright 1936 by Paul Leyssac, courtesy Mary Rehan.

Carolyn Bailey Hill: "The Teeny, Tiny Lady" from *Firelight Stories* by Carolyn Sherwin Bailey, copyright by Carolyn Bailey Hill.

Henry Holt & Company, Inc.: "Talk" from *The Cow-Tail Switch* by Harold Courlander and George Herzog, copyright 1947 by Henry Holt.

Hyperion Press: "The Goose that Laid the Golden Egg," "The Maid and the Milk Can," "The Dog and the Bone," and "The Farmer, His Son, and the Donkey," from *Aesop's Fables*, edited and rewritten by Elizabeth Stones and illustrated by Emery Kelen, copyright 1944 by The Hyperion Press.

Little, Brown & Company: "Cinderella," special version by Katharine Gibson, from the Tenggren *Tell-It-Again* book, copyright 1942 by The Artists and Writers Guild, Inc.

Thomas Nelson & Sons: "Salt" from *Old Peter's Russian Tales* by Arthur Ransome.

Pantheon Books, Inc.: "The Bremen Town Musicians" and "Rapunzel" from *Grimm's Fairy Tales*, retold by James Stern, based on Margaret Hunt's translation, copyright 1944 by Pantheon Books, Inc.

G. P. Putnam's Sons: "The Little Red Hen and the Grain of Wheat" from *Chimney Corner Stories*, edited by V. S. Hutchinson.

Row, Peterson & Company: "Three Billy Goats Gruff" from *East o' the Sun and West o' the Moon* by Gudrun Thorne-Thomsen.

FAVORITE NURSERY STORIES

The Little Red Hen and the Grain of Wheat

Retold by VERONICA S. HUTCHINSON

ONE DAY the Little Red Hen was scratching in the farmyard, when she found a grain of wheat.

"Who will plant the wheat?" said she.

"Not I," said the duck.
"Not I," said the cat.
"Not I," said the dog.

"Very well then," said the Little Red Hen, "I will." So she

THE LITTLE RED HEN planted the grain of wheat.

After some time the wheat grew tall and ripe.
"Who will cut the wheat?" asked the Little Red Hen.

"Not I," said the duck.
"Not I," said the cat.
"Not I," said the dog.

"Very well then, I will," said the Little Red Hen. So she cut the wheat.

"Now," she said, "who will thresh the wheat?"

"Not I," said the duck.
"Not I," said the cat.
"Not I," said the dog.

"Very well then, I will," said the Little Red Hen. So she threshed the wheat.

When the wheat was threshed, she said, "Who will take the wheat to the mill to have it ground into flour?"

"Not I," said the duck.
"Not I," said the cat.
"Not I," said the dog.

"Very well then, I will," said the Little Red Hen. So she took the wheat to the mill.

When the wheat was ground into flour, she said, "Who will make this flour into bread?"

"Not I," said the duck.
"Not I," said the cat.
"Not I," said the dog.

"Very well then, I will," said the Little Red Hen, and then baked a lovely loaf of bread.

Then she said, "Who will eat the bread?"

"Oh! I will," said the duck.
"Oh! I will," said the cat.
"Oh! I will," said the dog.

"Oh, no, you won't!" said the Little Red Hen. "I will." And she called her chicks and shared the bread with them.

From *Chimney Corner Stories*

The Old Woman and Her Pig

Retold by JOSEPH JACOBS

AN OLD WOMAN was sweeping her house, and she found a little crooked sixpence. "What," said she, "shall I do with this little sixpence? I will go to market, and buy a little pig."

As she was coming home, she came to a stile, but the piggy wouldn't go over the stile.

She went a little farther, and she met a dog. So she said to him, "Dog! dog! bite pig; piggy won't go over the stile; and I shan't get home tonight." But the dog wouldn't.

She went a little farther and she met a stick. So she said, "Stick! stick! beat dog! dog won't bite pig; piggy won't get over the stile; and I shan't get home tonight." But the stick wouldn't.

She went a little farther, and she met a fire. So she said, "Fire! fire! burn stick; stick won't beat dog; dog won't bite pig; piggy won't get over the stile; and I shan't get home tonight." But the fire wouldn't.

She went a little farther, and she met some water. So she said, "Water! water! quench fire; fire won't burn stick; stick won't beat dog; dog won't bite pig; piggy won't get over the stile; and I shan't get home tonight." But the water wouldn't.

She went a little farther, and she met an ox. So she said, "Ox! ox! drink water; water won't quench fire; fire won't burn stick; stick won't beat dog; dog won't bite pig; piggy won't get over the stile; and I shan't get home tonight." But the ox wouldn't.

She went a little farther, and she met a butcher. So she said, "Butcher! butcher! kill ox; ox won't drink water; water won't quench fire; fire won't burn stick; stick won't beat dog; dog won't bite pig; piggy won't get over the stile; and I shan't get home tonight." But the butcher wouldn't.

THE OLD WOMAN AND HER PIG

She went a little farther, and she met a rope. So she said, "Rope! rope! hang butcher; butcher won't kill ox; ox won't drink water; water won't quench fire; fire won't burn stick; stick won't beat dog; dog won't bite pig; piggy won't get over the stile; and I shan't get home tonight." But the rope wouldn't.

She went a little farther, and she met a rat. So she said, "Rat! rat! gnaw rope; rope won't hang butcher; butcher won't kill ox; ox won't drink water; water won't quench fire; fire won't burn stick; stick won't beat dog; dog won't bite pig; piggy won't get over the stile; and I shan't get home tonight." But the rat wouldn't.

She went a little farther, and she met a cat. So she said, "Cat! cat! kill rat; rat won't gnaw rope; rope won't hang butcher; butcher won't kill ox; ox won't drink water; water won't quench fire; fire won't burn stick; stick won't beat dog; dog won't bite pig; piggy won't get over the stile; and I shan't get home tonight."

But the cat said to her, "If you will go to yonder cow, and fetch me a saucer of milk, I will kill the rat." So away went the old woman to the cow.

But the cow said to her, "If you will go to yonder haystack, and fetch me a handful of hay, I'll give you the milk." So away went the old woman to the haystack; and she brought the hay.

As soon as the cow had eaten the hay, she gave the old woman

the milk; and away she went with it in a saucer to the cat.

As soon as the cat had lapped up the milk, the cat began to kill the rat; the rat began to gnaw the rope; the rope began to hang the butcher; the butcher began to kill the ox; the ox began to drink the water; the water began to quench the fire; the fire began to burn the stick; the stick began to beat the dog; the dog began to bite the pig; the little pig in a fright jumped over the stile; and so the old woman got home that night.

From *English Fairy Tales*

Goldilocks and the Three Bears

ONCE upon a time there were three Bears who lived in a little house in the woods. There was a Great Big Father Bear, with a great big voice, and a Middle-Sized Mother Bear, with a middle-sized voice, and a Little Wee Baby Bear, with a little, wee voice.

One morning the three Bears had porridge for breakfast, and the Mother Bear said,

"This porridge is too hot to eat now. Let us go to the woods for a walk, while the porridge gets cold."

So the three Bears went for a walk in the woods.

Now while they were gone, along came a little girl named Goldilocks. When she saw the little house in the woods she wondered who lived there, so she knocked at the door. No one answered, so she knocked again. Still no one answered, so Goldilocks opened the door and walked in.

There before her, in the little room, she saw a table set for three. There was a great big bowl of porridge, a middle-sized bowl of porridge, and a little, wee bowl of porridge. She tasted the great big bowl of porridge.

"Oh, this is too hot!" she said.

Then she tasted the middle-sized bowl of porridge.

"Oh, this is too cold!"

Then she tasted the little, wee bowl of porridge.

"Oh, this is just right!" she said, and ate it all up.

Then she went into another room, and there she saw three

chairs. There was a great big chair and a middle-sized chair and a little, wee chair. Goldilocks sat down in the great big chair.

'Oh, this is too hard!" she said.

Then she sat down in the middle-sized chair.

"Oh, this is too soft!"

Then she sat in the little, wee chair.

"Oh, this is just right!" and she sat down so hard that she sat the bottom out.

Then she went into another room, and there she saw three beds. There was a great big bed and a middle-sized bed and a little, wee bed. Goldilocks lay down on the great big bed.

"Oh, this is too hard!" she said.

Then she tried the middle-sized bed.

"Oh, this is too soft!"

Then she tried the little, wee bed.

"Oh, this is just right!" she sighed, and fell fast asleep.

Now while Goldilocks was asleep, the three Bears returned from their walk in the woods. They looked at the table, and the Great Big Father Bear said, in his great big voice,

"SOMEONE HAS BEEN TASTING MY PORRIDGE."

The Middle-Sized Mother Bear said, in her middle-sized voice,

"SOMEONE HAS BEEN TASTING MY PORRIDGE."

And the Little Wee Baby Bear said, in his little, wee voice,

"Someone has been tasting my porridge and has eaten it all up!"

Then the three Bears went into the next room. The Great Big Father Bear looked at his chair and said, in his great big voice,

"SOMEONE HAS BEEN SITTING IN MY CHAIR."

Then the Middle-Sized Mother Bear said in her middle-sized voice,

"SOMEONE HAS BEEN SITTING IN MY CHAIR."

And the Little Wee Baby Bear cried, in his little, wee voice,

"Someone has been sitting in my chair, and has sat the bottom out!"

Then the three Bears went into their bedroom. The Great Big Father Bear said, in his great big voice,

"SOMEONE HAS BEEN LYING IN MY BED."

And the Middle-Sized Mother Bear said, in her middle-sized voice,

"SOMEONE HAS BEEN LYING IN MY BED."

And the Little Wee Baby Bear cried, in his little, wee voice,

"Someone has been lying in my bed, and here she is!"

Now the shrill voice of the Little Wee Baby Bear waked Goldilocks, and you may well believe she was frightened to see the three Bears looking at her. She jumped from the bed, ran across the room, sprang out of the little, low window, and away she ran through the woods as fast as ever her legs could carry her.

The Three Little Pigs

Retold by JOSEPH JACOBS

THERE was an old sow with three little pigs, and as she had not enough to keep them, she sent them out to seek their fortune. The first that went off met a man with a bundle of straw, and said to him,

"Please, man, give me that straw to build me a house."

Which the man did, and the little pig built a house with it. Presently came along a wolf, and knocked at the door, and said,

"Little pig, little pig, let me come in."

To which the pig answered,

"No, no, by the hair of my chinny chin chin."

The wolf then answered to that,

"Then I'll huff, and I'll puff, and I'll blow your house in."

So he huffed, and he puffed, and he blew the house in, and ate up the little pig.

The second little pig met a man who was carrying a bundle of brush, and said,

"Please, man, give me that brush to build a house."

Which the man did, and the pig built his house. Then along came the wolf, and said,

"Little pig, little pig, let me come in."

"No, no, by the hair of my chinny chin chin."

"Then I'll puff, and I'll huff, and I'll blow your house in."

So he huffed, and he puffed, and he puffed, and he huffed, and at last he blew the house down, and he ate up the little pig.

The third little pig met a man with a load of bricks, and said,

"Please, man, give me those bricks to build a house with."

So the man gave him the bricks, and he built his house with them. So the wolf came, as he did to the other little pigs, and said,

"Little pig, little pig, let me come in."

"No, no, by the hair of my chinny chin chin."

"Then I'll huff, and I'll puff, and I'll blow your house in."

Well, he huffed, and he puffed, and he huffed, and he puffed, and he puffed and huffed; but he could *not* get the house down. When he found that he could not, with all his huffing and puffing, blow the house down, he said,

"Little pig, I know where there is a nice field of turnips."

"Where?" asked the little pig.

"Oh, in Mr. Smith's Home-field, and if you will be ready to-morrow morning, I will call for you, and we will go together, and get some for dinner."

"Very well," said the little pig, "I will be ready. What time do you mean to go?"

"Oh, at six o'clock."

Well, the little pig got up at five, and got the turnips before the wolf came (which he did about six), and said,

"Little pig, are you ready?"

The little pig said, "Ready! I have been and come back again, and got a nice potful for dinner."

The wolf felt very angry at this, but thought that he would be able to trap the little pig somehow or other, so he said,

"Little pig, I know where there is a nice apple tree."

"Where?" asked the pig.

"Down at Merry-garden," replied the wolf, "and if you will not deceive me I will come for you at five o'clock tomorrow and we shall get some apples."

Well, the little pig bustled up the next morning at four o'clock, and went off for the apples, hoping to get back before the wolf came. But he had farther to go, and had to climb the tree, so that just as he was coming down from it, he saw the

wolf coming, which, as you may suppose, frightened him very much. When the wolf came up he said,

"Little pig, are you here before me? Are they nice apples?"

"Yes, very nice," said the little pig. "I will throw you one."

And he threw it so far, that, while the wolf was gone to pick it up, the little pig jumped down and ran home. The next day the wolf came again, and said to the little pig,

"Little pig, there is a fair this afternoon. Will you go?"

"Oh yes," said the pig, "I will go. What time will you be ready?"

"At three," said the wolf. So the little pig went off before the time as usual, and got to the fair, and bought a butter-churn. He was carrying it home when he saw the wolf coming. So he got into the churn to hide, and by so doing turned it round, and it rolled down the hill with the pig in it. This frightened the wolf so much that he ran home without going to the fair. He went to the little pig's house, and told him how frightened he had been by a great round thing which came past him. Then the little pig said,

"Ha, I frightened you, then. I had been to the fair and bought a butter-churn, and when I saw you, I got into it, and rolled down the hill."

Then the wolf was very angry indeed, and declared he *would* eat up the little pig, and that he would climb down the chimney after him. When the little pig saw what he was about to do, he put on a pot full of water, and made up a blazing fire, and, just as the wolf was coming down, took off the cover. In fell the wolf; so the little pig put on the cover again in an instant, boiled him up, and ate him for supper.

The Wolf and the Seven Little Kids

By Jakob and Wilhelm Grimm

THERE was once upon a time an old goat who had seven little kids, and loved them with all the love of a mother for her children. One day she wanted to go into the forest and fetch some food. So she called all seven to her and said, "Dear children, I have to go into the forest. Be on your guard against the wolf. If he comes in, he will devour you all—skin, hair, and everything. The wretch often disguises himself, but you will know him at once by his rough voice and his black feet."

The kids said, "Dear mother, we will take good care of ourselves. You may go away without any anxiety." Then the old one bleated, and went on her way with an easy mind.

It was not long before someone knocked at the door and called, "Open the door, dear children. Your mother is here, and has brought something back with her for each of you."

But the little kids knew that it was the wolf, by the rough voice.

"We will not open the door,"cried they."You are not our mother. She has a soft, pleasant voice, but your voice is rough. You are the wolf!"

Then the wolf went away to a shopkeeper and bought himself a great lump of chalk, ate this, and made his voice soft with it. Then he came back, knocked at the door of the house, and cried, "Open the door, dear children. Your mother is here and has brought something back with her for each of you."

But the wolf had laid his black paws against the window, and the children saw them and cried, "We will not open the door. Our mother has not black feet like you. You are the wolf!"

Then the wolf ran to a baker and said, "I have hurt my feet. Rub some dough over them for me." And when the baker had rubbed his feet with the dough, he ran to the miller and said, "Strew some white meal over my feet for me." The miller thought to himself, "The wolf wants to deceive someone," and refused. But the

wolf said, "If you will not do it, I will devour you." Then the miller was afraid and made his paws white for him. Truly men are like that!

So now the wretch went for the third time to the house-door, knocked at it, and said, "Open the door for me, children. Your dear little mother has come home, and has brought every one of you something back from the forest with her."

The little kids cried, "First, show us your paws that we may know if you are our dear little mother."

Then he put his paws in through the window, and when the kids saw that they were white, they believed that all he said was true and opened the door. But who should come in but the wolf! They were terrified and wanted to hide themselves. One sprang under the table, the second into the bed, the third into the stove, the fourth into the kitchen, the fifth into the cupboard, the sixth under the washbowl, and the seventh into the clock case. But the wolf found them all and, one after the other, he swallowed

them down his throat. The youngest in the clock case was the only one he did not find.

When the wolf had satisfied his appetite, he took himself off, laid himself down under a tree in the green meadow outside, and began to sleep. Soon afterwards the old goat came home again from the forest. Ah, what a sight she saw there! The door stood wide open. The table, chairs, and benches were thrown down, the washbowl lay broken to pieces, and the quilts and pillows were pulled off the bed. She sought her children, but they were nowhere to be found. She called them one after another by name, but no one answered.

At last, when she came to the youngest, a soft voice cried, "Dear Mother, I am in the clock case." She took the kid out, and he told her that the wolf had come and had eaten all the others. Then you may imagine how she wept over her poor children.

At length in her grief she went out, and the youngest kid ran with her. When they came to the meadow, there lay the wolf by the tree. He snored so loud that the branches shook. She saw that something was moving and struggling in his gorged body.

"Ah, heavens," said she, "is it possible that my poor children, whom he has swallowed for his supper, can be still alive?"

Then the kid had to run home and fetch scissors and a needle and thread, and the goat cut open the monster's stomach. Hardly had she made one cut, than one little kid thrust his head out. When she had cut farther, all six sprang out one after another. What rejoicing there was! Then they embraced their dear mother, and jumped like a tailor at his wedding.

The mother, however, said, "Now go and look for some big stones, and we will fill the wicked beast's stomach with them while he is still asleep." Then the seven kids dragged the stones thither with all speed and put as many of them into his stomach as they could get in. The mother sewed him up again in the greatest haste, so that he was not aware of anything and never once stirred.

When the wolf at length had had his sleep out, he got on his legs. As the stones in his stomach made him very thirsty, he wanted to go to a well to drink. But when he began to walk and to move about, the stones in his stomach knocked against each other and rattled. Then cried he,

"What rumbles and tumbles
Against my poor bones?
I thought 'twas six kids,
But it's naught but big stones."

And when he got to the well and stooped over, the heavy stones made him fall in and he drowned miserably. When the seven kids saw that, they cried aloud, "The wolf is dead! The wolf is dead!" and danced for joy round about the well.

From Grimm's *Household Tales*,
translated by Margaret Hunt

Teeny, Tiny Lady

Retold by Carolyn Sherwin Bailey

ONCE upon a time there was a teeny, tiny lady who lived in a teeny, tiny house in a teeny, tiny village.

One day this teeny, tiny lady put on her teeny, tiny bonnet, and tied the teeny, tiny strings under her teeny, tinv chin, for she thought she would go for a teeny, tiny walk.

So she walked, and walked, and she came to a teeny, tiny gate which led into a teeny, tiny field. The teeny, tiny lady opened the gate, and walked into the field, and there, at the foot of a teeny, tiny tree, sat a teeny, tiny hen.

"This teeny, tiny hen will lay me a teeny, tiny egg for my teeny, tiny breakfast," said the teeny, tiny lady; so she took the teeny, tiny hen, and put her in her teeny, tiny reticule, and she went home again.

But when she came to her teeny, tiny house, she felt a teeny, tiny bit tired, so she put the teeny, tiny hen in her teeny, tiny cupboard, and she went upstairs to take a teeny, tiny nap.

And she had not been asleep so very long when she heard a

teeny, tiny voice which woke her, and it said,

"Give me my hen."

Then the teeny, tiny lady was a teeny, tiny bit afraid, but she pulled the teeny, tiny quilt up to her teeny, tiny chin and she went to sleep again.

But soon she heard the teeny, tiny voice again, and it said a little louder,

"Give me my hen!"

Then the teeny, tiny lady was a teeny, tiny bit more afraid, but she hid her teeny, tiny head in her teeny, tiny quilt, and she went to sleep again.

But very soon the voice called again, very loud,

"GIVE ME MY HEN!"

Then the teeny, tiny lady sat up in bed, and she called out in a loud teeny, tiny voice,

"TAKE IT!"

And when it came morning, the teeny, tiny lady went downstairs, and looked in her teeny, tiny cupboard; and what do you think? The teeny, tiny hen was gone!

From *Firelight Stories*

The Pancake

Retold by GEORGE WEBBE DASENT

ONCE on a time there was a good woman who had seven hungry children, and she was frying a pancake for them. It was a sweet-milk pancake, and there it lay in the pan bubbling and frizzling so thick and good, it was a sight for sore eyes to look at. And the children stood round about, and the good-man sat by and looked on.

"Oh, give me a bit of pancake, Mother, dear; I am so hungry," said one child.

"Oh, darling Mother," said the second.

"Oh, darling, good Mother," said the third.

"Oh, darling, good, nice Mother," said the fourth.

"Oh, darling, pretty, good, nice Mother," said the fifth.

"Oh, darling, pretty, good, nice, clever Mother," said the sixth.

"Oh, darling, pretty, good, nice, clever, sweet Mother," said the seventh.

So they begged for the pancake all round, the one more prettily than the other, for they were so hungry.

"Yes, yes, children, only wait a bit till the pancake turns itself" —she ought to have said, "till I can get it turned"—"and then you shall have some—a lovely sweet-milk pancake. Only look how fat and happy it lies there."

When the pancake heard that, it got afraid, and in a trice it turned itself all of itself, and tried to jump out of the pan, but dropped back into it again t'other side up. And so when it had been fried a little on the other side too, till it got firmer in its flesh, it sprang out on the floor, and rolled off like a wheel through the door and down the hill.

"Holloa! Stop, pancake!" and away went the good woman after it, with the frying pan in one hand and the ladle in the other, as fast as she could, and her children behind her, while the goodman limped after them last of all.

"Hi! Won't you stop? Seize it. Stop, pancake," they all screamed out, one after the other, and tried to catch it on the run and hold it. But the pancake rolled on and on, and in the twinkling of an eye it was so far ahead that they couldn't see it, for the pancake

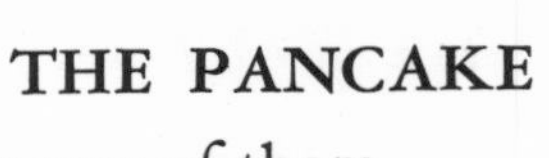

was faster than any of them.

So when it had rolled awhile it met a man.

"Good day, pancake," said the man.

"God bless you, Manny Panny!" said the pancake.

"Dear pancake," said the man, "don't roll so fast. Stop a little and let me eat you."

"When I have given the slip to Goody Poody, and the goodman, and seven squalling children, I may well slip through your fingers, Manny Panny," said the pancake, and rolled on and on till it met a hen.

"Good day, pancake," said the hen.

"The same to you, Henny Penny," said the pancake.

"Pancake, dear, don't roll so fast. Bide a bit and let me eat you up," said the hen.

"When I have given the slip to Goody Poody, and the goodman, and seven squalling children, and Manny Panny, I may well slip through your claws, Henny Penny," said the pancake, and so it rolled on like a wheel down the road.

Just then it met a cock.

"Good day, pancake," said the cock.

"The same to you, Cocky Locky," said the pancake.

"Pancake, dear, don't roll so fast, but bide a bit and let me eat you up."

"When I have given the slip to Goody Poody, and the goodman, and seven squalling children, and to Manny Panny, and Henny Penny, I may well slip through your claws, Cocky Locky," said the pancake, and off it set rolling away as fast as it could. And when it had rolled a long way it met a duck.

"Good day, pancake," said the duck.

"The same to you, Ducky Lucky."

"Pancake, dear, don't roll away so fast. Bide a bit and let me eat you up."

"When I have given the slip to Goody Poody, and the goodman, and seven squalling children, and Manny Panny, and Henny Penny, and Cocky Locky, I may well slip through your fingers, Ducky Lucky," said the pancake. With that it rolled faster than ever; and when it had rolled a long, long while, it met a goose.

"Good day, pancake," said the goose.

"The same to you, Goosey Poosey."

"Pancake, dear, don't roll so fast. Bide a bit and let me eat you up."

"When I have given the slip to Goody Poody, and the goodman, and seven squalling children, and Manny Panny, and Henny Penny, and Cocky Locky, and Ducky Lucky, I can well slip through your feet, Goosey Poosey," said the pancake, and off it rolled.

So when it had rolled a long, long way farther, it met a gander.

"Good day, pancake," said the gander.

"The same to you, Gander Pander," said the pancake.

"Pancake, dear, don't roll so fast. Bide a bit and let me eat you up."

"When I have given the slip to Goody Poody, and the goodman, and seven squalling children, and Manny Panny, and Henny Penny, and Cocky Locky, and Ducky Lucky, and Goosey Poosey, I may well slip through your feet, Gander Pander," said the pancake, which rolled off as fast as ever.

So when it had rolled a long, long time, it met a pig.

"Good day, pancake," said the pig.

"The same to you, Piggy Wiggy," said the pancake, which, without a word more, began to roll and roll like mad.

"Nay, nay," said the pig, "you needn't be in such a hurry. We two can go side by side and see each other over the wood. They say it is not too safe in there."

The pancake thought there might be something in that, and so they kept company. When they had gone a short distance, they came to a brook. As for Piggy, he was so fat he swam safely across; it was nothing to him. But the poor pancake couldn't get over.

"Seat yourself on my snout," said the pig, "and I'll carry you over."

So the pancake did that.

"Ouf, ouf," said the pig, and swallowed the pancake at one gulp. And then, as the poor pancake could go no farther, why—this story can go no farther either.

The Three Billy Goats Gruff

Retold by GUDRUN THORNE-THOMSEN

ONCE on a time there were three Billy Goats, who were to go up to the hillside to make themselves fat, and the family name of the goats was "Gruff."

On the way up was a bridge, over a river which they had to cross, and under the bridge lived a great ugly Troll with eyes as big as saucers and a nose as long as a poker.

First of all came the youngest Billy Goat Gruff to cross the bridge. "Trip, trap; trip, trap!" went the bridge.

"Who's that tripping over my bridge?" roared the Troll.

"Oh, it is only I, the tiniest Billy Goat Gruff, and I'm going up to the hillside to make myself fat," said the Billy Goat, with such a small voice.

"Now, I'm coming to gobble you up," said the Troll.

"Oh, no, pray do not take me. I'm too little, that I am," said the Billy Goat. "Wait a bit till the second Billy Goat Gruff comes, he's much bigger."

"Well, be off with you," said the Troll.

A little while after came the second Billy Goat Gruff across the bridge.

"Trip, trap! Trip, trap!" went the bridge.

"Who is that tripping over my bridge?" roared the Troll.

"Oh, it's the second Billy Goat Gruff, and I'm going up to the hillside to make myself fat," said the Billy Goat. Nor had he such a small voice either.

"Now, I'm coming to gobble you up!" said the Troll.

"Oh, no, don't take me. Wait a little till the big Billy Goat comes, he's much bigger."

"Very well! Be off with you," said the Troll.

But just then up came the big Billy Goat Gruff.

"Trip, trap! Trip, trap! Trip, trap!" went the bridge, for the Billy Goat was so heavy that the bridge creaked and groaned under him.

"Who's that tramping on my bridge?" roared the Troll.

"It is I! The big Billy Goat Gruff," said the Billy Goat, and he had a big hoarse voice.

"Now, I'm coming to gobble you up!" roared the Troll.

"Well come! I have two spears so stout,
With them I'll thrust your eyeballs out;
I have besides two great big stones,
With them I'll crush you body and bones!"

That was what the big Billy Goat said; so he flew at the Troll, and thrust him with his horns, and tossed him out into the river, and after that he went up to the hillside.

There the Billy Goats got so fat that they were scarcely able to walk home again. And if they haven't grown thinner, why they're still fat; and so,

"Snip, snap, stout.
This tale's told out."

From *East o' the Sun and West o' the Moon*

The Tale of Peter Rabbit

BY BEATRIX POTTER

ONCE upon a time there were four little Rabbits, and their names were Flopsy, Mopsy, Cotton-Tail, and Peter. They lived with their mother in a sandbank, underneath the root of a very big fir tree.

"Now, my dears," said old Mrs. Rabbit one morning, "you may go into the fields or down the lane, but don't go into Mr. McGregor's garden. Your Father had an accident there; he was put in a pie by Mrs. McGregor. Now run along, and don't get into mischief. I am going out."

Then old Mrs. Rabbit took a basket and her umbrella and went through the wood to the baker's. She bought a loaf of brown bread and five currant buns.

Flopsy, Mopsy, and Cotton-Tail, who were good little bunnies, went down the lane to gather blackberries.

But Peter, who was very naughty, ran straight away to Mr. McGregor's garden, and squeezed under the gate!

First he ate some lettuce and some French beans; and then he had some radishes. And then, feeling rather sick, he went to look for some parsley.

But round the end of a cucumber frame, whom should he meet but Mr. McGregor!

Mr. McGregor was on his hands and knees planting young cabbages, but he jumped up and ran after Peter, waving a rake and calling out, "Stop, thief!"

Peter was most dreadfully frightened. He rushed all over the garden, for he had forgotten the way back to the gate. He lost one of his shoes among the cabbages, and the other among the potatoes.

After losing them, he ran on four legs and went faster, so that I think he might have got away altogether if he had not unfortunately run into a gooseberry net, and got caught by the large buttons on his jacket. It was a blue jacket with brass buttons, quite new.

Peter gave himself up for lost, and shed big tears. But his sobs were overheard by some friendly sparrows, who flew to him in great excitement and implored him to exert himself.

Mr. McGregor came up with a sieve, which he intended to pop upon the top of Peter; but Peter wriggled out just in time, leaving his jacket behind him. And he rushed into the tool shed, and jumped into a can. It would have been a beautiful thing to hide in, if it had not had so much water in it.

Mr. McGregor was quite sure that Peter was somewhere in the tool shed, perhaps hidden underneath a flowerpot. He began to turn them over carefully, looking under each.

Presently Peter sneezed,

"Kerty-schoo!" Mr. McGregor was after him in no time, and tried to put his foot upon Peter, who jumped out of a window, upsetting three plants. The window was too small for Mr. McGregor, and he was tired of running after Peter. He went back to his work.

Peter sat down to rest. He was out of breath and trembling with fright, and he had not the least idea which way to go. Also, he was very damp with sitting in that can.

After a time he began to wander about, going lippity—lippity—not very fast, and looking all around.

He found a door in a wall; but it was locked, and there was no room for a fat little rabbit to squeeze underneath.

An old mouse was running in and out over the stone doorstep, carrying peas and beans to her family in the wood. Peter asked her the way to the gate, but she had such a large pea in her mouth that she could not answer. She only shook her head at him. Peter began to cry.

Then he tried to find his way straight across the garden, but he became more and more puzzled. Presently, he came to a pond where Mr. McGregor filled his water cans. A white cat was staring at some goldfish. She sat very, very still, but now and then the tip of her tail twitched as if it were alive. Peter thought it best to go away without speaking to her; he had heard about cats from his cousin, little Benjamin Bunny.

He went back toward the tool shed, but suddenly, quite close to him, he heard the noise of a hoe—scr-r-ritch, scratch, scratch, scritch. Peter scuttered underneath the bushes. But presently, as nothing happened, he came out, and climbed upon a wheelbarrow and peeped over. The first thing he saw was Mr. McGregor hoeing onions. His back was turned toward Peter, and beyond him was the gate!

Peter got down very quietly off the wheelbarrow, and started running as fast as he could go, along a straight walk behind some black-currant bushes.

Mr. McGregor caught sight of him at the corner, but Peter did not care. He slipped underneath the gate, and was safe at last in the wood outside the garden.

Mr. McGregor hung up the little jacket and the shoes for a

scarecrow to frighten the blackbirds.

Peter never stopped running or looked behind him till he got home to the big fir tree.

He was so tired that he flopped down upon the nice soft sand on the floor of the rabbit hole, and shut his eyes.

His mother was busy cooking; she wondered what he had done with his clothes. It was the second little jacket and pair of shoes that Peter had lost in a fortnight!

I am sorry to say that Peter was not very well during the evening.

His mother put him to bed and made some camomile tea; and she gave a dose of it to Peter!

"One tablespoonful to be taken at bedtime."

But Flopsy, Mopsy, and Cotton-Tail had bread and milk and blackberries for supper.

From *The Tale of Peter Rabbit*

The Bremen Town Musicians

By Jakob and Wilhelm Grimm

A CERTAIN MAN had a donkey, which had carried the corn sacks to the mill for many a long year; but his strength was going, and he was growing more and more unfit for work. Then his master began to consider how he might best save his keep; but the donkey, seeing that no good wind was blowing, ran away and set out on the road to Bremen.

"There," he thought, "I can surely be town musician." When he had walked some distance, he found a hound lying on the road, gasping like one who had run till he was tired. "What are you gasping so for, you big fellow?" asked the donkey.

"Ah," replied the hound, "as I am old, and daily grow weaker, and no longer can hunt, my master wanted to kill me, so I took to flight. But now how am I to earn my bread?"

"I tell you what," said the donkey, "I am going to Bremen, and shall be town musician there. Go with me and engage yourself also as a musician. I will play the lute, and you shall beat the kettledrum."

The hound agreed, and on they went.

Before long they came to a cat, sitting on the path, with a face like three rainy days! "Now then, old shaver, what has gone askew with you?" asked the donkey.

"Who can be merry when his neck is in danger?" answered the cat. "Because I am now getting old, and my teeth are worn to stumps, and I prefer to sit by the fire, rather than hunt about after mice, my mistress wanted to drown me, so I ran away. But now good advice is scarce. Where am I to go?"

"Go with us to Bremen. You understand night music, so you can be a town musician."

The cat thought well of it, and went with them. After this the three fugitives came to a farmyard, where the cock was sitting upon the gate, crowing with all his might. "Your crow goes through and through one," said the donkey. "What is the matter?"

"I have been foretelling fine weather," said the cock. "But guests are coming for Sunday, so the housewife has no pity, and has told the cook that she intends to eat me in the soup tomorrow, and this evening I am to have my head cut off. Now I am crowing at the top of my lungs while still I can."

"Ah, but red-comb," said the donkey, "you had better come away with us. We are going to Bremen. You have a good voice, and if we make music together it must have some quality!"

The cock agreed to this plan, and all four went on together. They could not reach the city of Bremen in one day, however, and in the evening they came to a forest where they meant to pass the night. The donkey and the hound laid themselves down under a large tree. The cat and the cock settled themselves in the branches; but the cock flew right to the top, where he was most safe. Before he went to sleep he looked round on all four sides, and thought he saw in the distance a little spark burning. So he called out to his companions that there must be a house not far off, for he saw a light.

The donkey said, "If so, we had better get up and go on, for the shelter here is bad." The hound thought, too, that a few bones with some meat on would do him good!

So they made their way to the place where the light was, and soon saw it shine brighter and grow larger, until they came to a well-lighted robbers' house. The donkey, as the biggest, went to the window and looked in.

"What do you see, my gray-horse?" asked the cock.

"What do I see?" answered the donkey. "A table covered with good things to eat and drink, and robbers sitting at the table enjoying themselves."

"That would be the sort of thing for us," said the cock.

"Yes, yes. Ah, if only we were there!" said the donkey.

Then the animals took counsel together how they should manage to drive away the robbers, and at last they thought of a plan. The donkey was to place himself with his forefeet upon the window ledge, the hound was to jump on the donkey's back, the cat was to climb upon the dog, and the cock was to fly up on the head of the cat.

When this was done, at a given signal, they began to perform their music together: the donkey brayed, the hound barked, the cat mewed, and the cock crowed. Then they burst through the window into the room, shattering the glass! At this horrible din, the robbers sprang up, thinking no otherwise than that a ghost had come in, and fled in a great fright out into the forest. The four companions now sat down at the table, well content with what was left, and ate as if they were going to fast for a month.

As soon as the four minstrels had done, they put out the light, and each sought for himself a sleeping place according to his nature. The donkey laid himself down upon some straw in the yard, the hound behind the door, the cat upon the hearth near the warm ashes; and the cock perched himself upon a beam of the roof. Being tired from their long walk, they soon went to sleep.

When it was past midnight, the robbers saw from afar that the light was no longer burning in their house, and all appeared quiet. The captain said, "We ought not to have let ourselves be frightened out of our wits," and ordered one of them to go and examine the house.

The messenger, finding all still, went into the kitchen to light a candle. Taking the glistening, fiery eyes of the cat for live coals, he held a match to them to light it. But the cat did not understand the joke, and flew in his face, spitting and scratching. He was dreadfully frightened, and ran to the back door, but the dog,

who lay there, sprang up and bit his leg. As he ran across the yard, the donkey gave him a smart kick with his hind foot. The cock, too, who had been awakened by the noise, and had become lively, cried down from the beam, "Cock-a-doodle-doo!"

Then the robber ran back as fast as he could to his captain, and said, "Ah, there is a horrible witch sitting in the house, who spat on me and scratched my face with her long claws. By the door stands a man with a knife, who stabbed me in the leg. In the yard there lies a black monster, who beat me with a wooden club; and above, upon the roof, sits the judge, who called out 'Bring the rogue here to me!' so I got away as well as I could."

After this the robbers never again dared enter the house; but it suited the four musicians of Bremen so well that they did not care to leave it any more. And the mouth of him who last told this story is still warm.

From Grimm's *Fairy Tales*, retold by James Stern from Margaret Hunt's translation

The Shoemaker and the Elves

By Jakob and Wilhelm Grimm

THERE was once a shoemaker, who, through no fault of his own, became so poor that at last he had nothing left but just enough leather to make one pair of shoes. He cut out the shoes at night, so as to set to work on them the next morning; and, as he had a good conscience, he laid himself quietly down in his bed, committed himself to heaven, and fell asleep. In the morning, after he had said his prayers, and was going to get to work, he found the pair of shoes made and finished, and standing on his table. He was very much astonished, and did not know what to think.

After a moment, the poor man took the shoes in his hand to examine them more carefully, and found them so well made that every stitch was in its right place, just as if they had come from the hand of a master workman.

Soon after, a purchaser entered, and as the shoes fitted him very well, he gave more than the usual price for them, so that the shoemaker had enough money to buy leather for two more pairs of shoes. He cut out the shoes at night, and intended to set to work the next morning with fresh spirit. But that was not to be, for when he got up, the two pairs of shoes were already finished, and even a customer was not lacking, who gave him so much money that he was able to buy leather enough for four new pairs. Early next morning he found the four pairs also finished, and so it always happened. Whatever he cut out in the evening was worked up by the morning, so that he was soon in the way of making a good living, and in the end became very well-to-do.

One night, not long before Christmas, when the shoemaker had finished cutting out, and before he went to bed, he said to his wife,

"How would it be if we were to sit up tonight and see who it is that does us this service?"

His wife agreed and set a light to burn. They both hid in a corner of the room, behind some coats that were hanging up, and then they began to watch. As soon as it was midnight, they saw come in two neatly formed naked little men, who seated themselves before the shoemaker's table, and took up the work that was already prepared. They began to stitch, to pierce, and to hammer so cleverly and quickly with their little fingers that the shoemaker's eyes could scarcely follow them, so full of wonder was he. And they never left off until everything was finished and ready on the table, and then they jumped up and ran off.

The next morning the shoemaker's wife said to her husband, "Those little men have made us rich, and we ought to show ourselves grateful. With all their running about, and having nothing to cover them, they must be very cold. I'll tell you what: I will make little shirts, coats, waistcoats, and breeches for them, and knit each of them a pair of stockings, and you shall make each of them a pair of shoes."

The husband consented willingly, and at night, when everything was finished, they laid the gifts together on the table, instead of the cut-out work, and placed themselves so that they could observe how the little men would behave. When midnight came, they rushed in, ready to set to work, but when they found, instead of pieces of prepared leather, the neat little garments, they stood a moment in surprise, and then they showed the greatest delight. Swiftly they took up the pretty garments and slipped them on, singing,

What spruce and dandy boys are we!
No longer cobblers we will be.

Then they hopped and danced about, and at last they danced out at the door.

They were never seen again, but it went well with the shoemaker as long as he lived.

FOLK AND FAIRY TALES

Jack and the Beanstalk

Retold by Dinah M. Mulock Craik

IN THE DAYS of King Alfred, there lived a poor widow in a country village, many miles from London. She had an only child named Jack, who was lazy and extravagant, and, little by little, he spent nearly everything that she had. One day, for the first time in her life, she reproached him, "Cruel boy! I have not money enough to purchase even a bit of bread, nothing now remains but my poor cow!"

Jack teased his mother to let him sell the cow at the next village, and at last she consented.

As he was going along he met a butcher who held some curious beans in his hat. He offered them to Jack in exchange for the cow, and the silly boy could not conceal his pleasure at what he supposed so great an offer. The cow was exchanged for a few paltry beans, and Jack made his way home.

But when his mother saw the beans, her patience quite forsook her. She tossed the beans out of the window, where they fell in the garden below. Then she threw her apron over her head, and cried bitterly. Jack tried to comfort her, but in vain, and, not having anything to eat, they both went supperless to bed.

Jack awoke early in the morning, and saw that something was darkening the window of his room. When he ran downstairs into the garden, he found that some of the beans had taken root, and sprung up surprisingly. The stalks were very thick, and had twined together until they formed a ladder like a chain, and they were so high that the top appeared to be lost in the clouds. Jack was an adventurous lad, and he determined to climb up to the top.

After climbing for some hours, he found himself in a strange country. He walked on, and after a while he met a beautiful lady. She was elegantly clad, and carried a white wand, at the top of which sat a peacock of pure gold. With a bewitching smile, she asked him how he came there, and he told her about the beanstalk.

"Do you remember your father, young man?" the lady asked him.

"No, madam. My mother always begins to weep if I mention his name, and will tell me nothing."

"She dare not," replied the lady, "but I can and will. I am a fairy, and was your father's guardian. But fairies are bound by laws, as well as mortals, and, when I made a mistake, I lost my power for years. I was unable to help your father when he most needed it, and so he died." Here the fairy looked so sorrowful that Jack's heart warmed to her, and he begged her to tell him more.

"Your father was a most excellent man," the fairy continued.

"He had a good wife, faithful servants, and plenty of money. But he had one misfortune—a false friend, a giant, whom he had helped in misfortune. This giant returned your father's kindness by murdering him and seizing all his property. He also made your mother promise that she would never tell you what had happened, or he would murder both her and you. I could not help her. My power only returned on the day you went to sell your cow.

"It was I," added the fairy, "who made you decide to take the beans. It was I who made the beanstalk grow, and inspired you with the desire to climb up it to this strange country. The wicked giant lives here, and you must rid the world of a monster who never will do anything but evil. You may lawfully take possession of his house and all his riches, for everything he has belonged to your father, and is therefore yours. But do not let your mother know you are acquainted with your father's history."

Jack asked what he was to do next.

"Go along this road, until you see the house where the giant lives. Then act according to your own just judgment. And now farewell!"

The fairy vanished, and Jack walked on until after sunset, when, to his great joy, he saw a large mansion. A plain-looking woman was at the door, and he begged her to give him a morsel of bread and a night's lodging. She was surprised, and said it was quite uncommon to see a human being near their house. It was well known that her husband was a powerful giant, who would never eat anything but human flesh, if he could possibly get it.

Jack was terrified, but still he hoped to get the best of the giant. He again begged the woman to take him in for one night only, and to hide him where she thought proper. She finally agreed. They entered a fine large hall, and she led him to a room where she gave him plenty to eat and drink. He was just beginning to enjoy himself, when he was startled by a loud knocking at the outer door, which made the whole house shake.

"Ah, that's the giant. If he sees you, he will kill you and me too," cried the poor woman, trembling all over. "What shall I do?"

"Hide me in the oven," cried Jack. So he crept into the oven —for there was no fire near it—and listened to the giant's loud voice scolding his wife. At last he seated himself at the table, and Jack peeped through a crevice in the oven. The boy was amazed to see what a quantity of food the giant devoured. It seemed as if he would never finish eating and drinking, but he did at last. Leaning back, he called to his wife in a voice like thunder,

"Bring me my hen!"

She obeyed, and placed upon the table a very beautiful live hen.

"Lay!" roared the giant, and the hen laid immediately an egg of solid gold.

"Lay another!" Every time the giant said this, the hen laid a larger egg than before.

He amused himself a long time with his hen. Then he sent his wife to bed, while he fell asleep by the fireside and snored like the roaring of a cannon.

As soon as the giant was asleep, Jack crept out of the oven, seized the hen, and ran off with her. He ran down the road until he reached the top of the beanstalk, which he descended in safety. His mother was overjoyed to see him. She thought he had come to some ill end.

"Not a bit of it, Mother." He told her of his adventure, but was careful not to mention his father. Then he showed her the hen. "Now lay," he said, and the hen laid as many golden eggs as he desired.

After these eggs were sold, Jack and his mother had plenty of money. They lived happily together for some months. Then Jack began to long to climb the beanstalk again, and carry away some more of the giant's riches. He had a dress prepared which would disguise him, and something to color his skin. A few mornings after, he rose very early, before his mother was up, and climbed the beanstalk a second time. He continued his journey and reached the giant's mansion, late in the evening. The woman was at the door as before, and Jack asked her to give him some food.

She told him (what he knew very well) that her husband was a powerful and cruel giant. She also said that one night she had admitted a poor, hungry, friendless boy, and the ungrateful fellow had stolen one of the giant's treasures. Her husband had blamed her for this misfortune, and had treated her very cruelly ever since. Jack felt sorry for her, but confessed nothing, and did his best to persuade her to admit him. He found it a hard task, but at last she consented. She took him into the kitchen, and after he had finished eating and drinking, she hid him in an old closet.

The giant returned at the usual time, and walked in saying,

"Fee—fi—fo—fum,
I smell the blood of an Englishman,
Be he alive, or be he dead,
I'll grind his bones to make my bread."

The wife replied it was the crows, which had brought a piece of raw meat, and left it at the top of the house. While she was preparing supper, the giant was very ill-tempered, frequently lifting his hand to strike his wife for not being quick enough. And he scolded her again and again for the loss of his wonderful hen.

At last, having finished his supper, he cried, "Give me something to amuse me. Bring me my moneybags."

His wife brought them, staggering under the weight. There were two bags—one filled with new guineas, and the other with new shillings. She emptied them out on the table, and the giant began counting them in great glee. "Now you may go to bed, you old fool," he said, and the wife crept away.

From his hiding place, Jack watched the counting of the money. He knew it had belonged to his poor father and wished it was his own. The giant, little thinking he was being watched, finally put the money back in the two bags. He tied them up very carefully and set them beside his chair, with his little dog to guard them. At last he fell asleep, as before, and snored so loudly that Jack compared his noise to the roaring of the sea in a high wind. Jack stole out of his hiding place, but just as he laid his hand upon the two bags of money, the little dog started from under the giant's chair. It barked furiously and Jack stood still, expecting his enemy to awake any instant. Fortunately, the giant continued in a sound sleep. At that moment Jack saw a piece of meat, and threw it to the dog. It stopped barking to devour the meat, and

Jack carried off the bags, one on each shoulder. They were so heavy that it took him two whole days to climb down the beanstalk.

When he at last reached home, he gave his mother the two moneybags. They had the cottage rebuilt and well furnished, and lived more happily than they had ever done before.

For three years Jack said no more of the beanstalk, but he could not forget it. Finally, he began to make secret preparations for another journey. He got ready a new disguise, better and more complete than the one he had used before. When summer came, he woke on the longest day as soon as it was light. Without telling his mother, he climbed up the beanstalk, and he arrived at the giant's mansion in the evening. As usual the wife was standing at the door. Jack had disguised himself so completely, that she did not remember him at all. But when he pleaded hunger and poverty, in order to gain admittance, he found it very difficult to persuade her. At last she hid him in the copper.

When the giant returned, he said furiously,

"Fee—fi—fo—fum,
I smell the blood of an Englishman,
Be he alive, or be he dead,
I'll grind his bones to make my bread."

Then he searched the room. Jack was terrified. When the giant approached the copper he started to lift the lid. But he let it drop, sat down by the fireside, and began to eat his enormous supper. Then he called for his harp.

The giant placed it on the table, and said, "Play!" Then it played without anybody touching it. It was the most exquisite music, and Jack was more anxious to get this than any of his enemy's treasures. But the giant was not very fond of music, and the harp only lulled him to sleep. The wife had already gone to bed.

As soon as Jack thought all was safe, he got out of the copper. Seizing the harp, he started to run off with it. But the harp was enchanted, and as soon as it found itself in strange hands, it called out loudly, just as if it had been alive, "Master! Master!"

The giant awoke, started up, and saw Jack scampering away.

"Oh, you villain! It is you who have robbed me of my hen and my moneybags, and now you are stealing my harp also," he cried. "Wait till I catch you, and I'll eat you alive!"

"Very well, try!" shouted Jack. He saw the giant had eaten so much he could hardly stand, much less run; and he himself had young legs and a clear conscience, which carry a man a long way. So, after leading the giant quite a race, he managed to be first at the top of the beanstalk. He scrambled down it as fast as he could, the harp playing all the while the most melancholy music.

Arrived at the bottom, Jack found his mother sitting at her cottage door, weeping silently. She had been much worried.

"Here, Mother, don't cry," he said, "just give me a hatchet, make haste." He saw the giant beginning to descend the beanstalk, and he knew there was not a moment to spare.

But the monster's ill deeds had come to an end. Jack took his hatchet and cut the beanstalk close off at the root. The giant fell headlong into the garden, and was killed on the spot.

Instantly the fairy appeared, and explained everything to Jack's mother. So all ended well, and nothing was ever more heard or seen of the wonderful Beanstalk.

Adapted from *The Fairy Book*

Dick Whittington and His Cat

Retold by May Hill

LONG ago, in a small country village in England, there lived a boy named Dick Whittington. Dick's father and mother had died, and the boy had a hard time getting along by himself. The people of the town were poor working folk, with little enough for themselves, and still less to spare an orphan. Dick lived in rags and tatters, and never knew what it was to have enough to eat. In spite of his hard life, Dick was a bright, happy boy, dreaming great dreams of the fine life he would lead when he grew to be a man. He used to listen to stories about London, told by the postboys and wagoners who came from that city. I am afraid they found it good sport to make Dick's big eyes grow bigger with wonder, for they told him that all the people in London were rich and happy, with nothing to do but dance and make

merry. They told him the streets of London were paved with gold.

"Then," said Dick, "all I need to do is to walk to London, and there I can pick up enough gold to buy me some warm clothes and maybe a whole loaf of bread."

"That's right, my lad," the postboys would say, laughing among themselves, "but you will have to wait until your legs grow longer, for you could never walk to London as they are now."

"I suppose that is true," said poor Dick, sadly, and wondered how much longer his legs would have to grow before he could set off for London.

One bright spring day, after Dick had spent a very hard winter, there drove through the town a large wagon. It was drawn by eight fine horses with little bells tinkling at their heads. Dick had never seen so fine a sight, and when he heard they were bound for London he was greatly excited. He trotted along beside the wagoner, asking him many questions about the city. At last he summoned all his courage and asked the man to let him travel with them. At first the man said no. But when he learned that Dick had no home and was nearly starved, he thought Dick would be no worse off in London, so he let the little chap go along.

That must have been a hard journey for so small a boy. It was many miles, and they were many days on the road. The wagon was so heavily loaded with parcels and boxes that the wagoner had to walk in the road beside the horses, and Dick fell cheerfully into step with him.

At last the spires of London town came in sight. Dick was so excited that he could no longer go along as slowly as the wagoner and the horses. He thanked his friend, and set off on the run to find those London streets that were so wonderfully paved with gold. Poor Dick! Breathless and eager, he entered London, only to find in place of golden pavements and merry people, dirty streets and people looking more ragged and miserable than he. At first he could not believe his eyes, but wandered up and down, looking for the wonder and the beauty he had been led to expect. Finally, footsore, hungry, and wretched, Dick curled himself up in a dark corner and cried himself to sleep.

The next morning he was cold and hungry. He tried to beg a penny of the passers-by, but they hurried on without stopping to look at the little fellow who tugged at their coats. Dick tried all that day to get work, so that he might earn money and buy his food; but no one would take him, he looked so small and pale. That night he slept in the streets again. The next morning he was so weak with hunger that he could scarcely stand. He walked slowly along a street of fine houses, until he saw a fat cook come out of the door of one of the houses.

"Please, could you let me help you?" he asked. His legs shook so that he had to sit down on the steps to keep from falling.

"Help me, indeed, a lazy lump like you! Well, I should think not," said the cook.

Just then her master, Mr. Fitzwarren, came out of the house and asked kindly,

"What is the trouble, my boy?"

"Trouble enough, truly!" said Dick. "For two days I have been trying to get work and food, and now I am so weak and hungry I cannot stand up."

Mr. Fitzwarren was a kind man, and he felt sorry for Dick. So he took him into his house, gave him a good breakfast, and said he might stay with them and work for the cook. When the cook heard this, she was not too well pleased and, as she was very cross, Dick had a hard time of it. She used to say,

"When there are no eggs that need beating, there is always that lazy, good-for-nothing Dick."

The poor boy bore her ill treatment patiently, because he was thankful to Mr. Fitzwarren. One day little Alice Fitzwarren came into the kitchen suddenly and found the cook beating Dick. When the little girl found there was no reason for it, she told her father about the cook's cruelty, and Mr. Fitzwarren warned the woman that it must never occur again.

After that, life would have been very comfortable for Dick Whittington, except for one thing. The cook had housed him in an attic that was so overrun with rats and mice that the boy found it impossible to sleep at night. As soon as he had saved a penny he bought himself a cat and carried it to his attic to live with him there. The cat was a good mouser, and soon rid the place of rats, so Dick could sleep undisturbed. Dick became very fond of his cat; it was the only friend he seemed to have in those days. He named it "Tabby," and at night when his work was over he climbed up to his attic cheerfully, because he knew that he would find Tabby waiting for him. The cat would welcome him with a great purring and rubbing against him, and the two would curl

up on a bed of straw and go to sleep like two good friends.

One day Mr. Fitzwarren called all his servants together, and said to them, "My good ship 'Unicorn' is sailing tomorrow for foreign lands. It carries many things to be traded and sold. If each one of you will send something of your own on board my vessel, your venture may bring you good returns in gold or silver."

The servants thanked their master for thinking of them. Each one brought something to send overseas, except Dick. He sat very still, hoping that no one would notice him, but little Alice was in the room, and she called out,

"What are you sending, Dick Whittington?"

Poor Dick had to say that he had nothing to send.

"But you must have something of your own!" said Mr. Fitzwarren.

"Alas!" said Dick. "I have nothing in the world but my good cat Tabby."

"Then, my boy, you had better send the cat," urged Mr.

Fitzwarren. "You never can tell what will sell best in these strange foreign lands."

Poor Dick! Sorrowfully he climbed the stairs to his attic. Tabby bounded to the door to greet him, and purred loudly as he carried her downstairs. When Dick put her into Mr. Fitzwarren's arms, Tabby miaowed, as if she were not quite sure that all was well. The tears streamed down Dick's face as he stroked her head in farewell and told her she would probably find a better home than he had been able to give her.

All the servants laughed at this, but little Alice said, "Never mind, Dick, the captain will take good care of her, and I will give you some money to buy another cat."

So Tabby was carried away, and Dick was left feeling very lonely again. Worst of all, because Alice and Mr. Fitzwarren were kind to him, the cook grew angry and secretly mistreated him so cruelly that Dick felt he could not bear it. Time passed, and no word came from the "Unicorn." There was, indeed, a report that it had been lost at sea in a terrible storm. Dick wept to think that he had sent Tabby away.

One day the cook had been so tormenting and so cruel that Dick made up his mind to run away. The next morning, while it was still dark, he put his little bundle of clothes over his shoulder and set off, before anyone in the house was awake. He trudged along in the darkness as far as Holloway. There he sat down on a big rock, that to this day is called Whittington's stone. He rested there for a moment, wondering which road to take.

While he was sitting there the bells of Bow Church began to ring. Dick was startled, for in the stillness of the dawn they seemed to be pealing out words. He listened, and sure enough, the words sounded clearly:

> Turn again, Whittington,
> Thrice Lord Mayor of London town.
> Turn again, Whittington,
> Thrice Lord Mayor of London town.

"Lord Mayor of London!" thought Dick. "Well, to be sure, if I am to be Lord Mayor of London, it is nothing to me now that the cook ill-treats me. I can stand that and much worse, if in the end I am to be Mayor. I will turn back at once, and perhaps, if I hurry, I can get into the house before the cook misses me."

So for the second time Dick Whittington entered London, running as fast as his legs could carry him and with high hopes beating in his heart. This time he was lucky enough to avoid meeting the cook, and she never knew about his running away.

Weeks passed. Dick wondered secretly how in the world he was ever going to become Lord Mayor of London, if he continued to work for a bad-tempered old cook in the kitchen. One day there was great excitement in the Fitzwarren household. The captain of the "Unicorn" had come back. Mr. Fitzwarren sent for all the servants to come at once and hear the captain's strange tale.

Dick was very black from scouring pots and pans, but there was no time for him to wash, and besides, the spiteful old cook would not allow him to do so. As he edged his way into the room, he caught sight of little sacks of gold and silver on the table, and on the floor wonderful caskets of precious stones. But there was no sign of his beloved Tabby, and his heart was heavy. He shrank into a dim corner of the room, where no one could see him, and there he listened to the captain's story. This is what he heard:

"Our good ship 'Unicorn' was many days at sea, when we met with a terrible storm. We were driven off our course, until we knew not where we were. At last, after a week of storm and drifting in the fog, we sighted land. When we had made port, we went on shore and found ourselves in Barbary, among the Moors, a people we had never seen before. They received us kindly, and we sold and traded our cargo for better prices than we had ever received elsewhere. But now comes the strangest part of my tale.

"After we had disposed of all our goods, the servants of the King and Queen of Barbary, who had been buying for their monarchs, told us that the royal pair wished us to come to the palace. We were received in a splendid room, richly carpeted and hung with beautiful silks and brocades. The King and Queen were seated in front of them. Dinner was brought in, but as the servants placed the dishes before us, huge rats ran out from all sides, seized the food, and made off with it. We asked the King and Queen why they stood it, and the King replied,

" 'Stand it, indeed! Have I not offered half my treasure for anything that can rid us of these terrible pests? Still no one has found such a thing.'

"Of course, I was delighted when I heard this, so I told the King that if he would really keep his word and give half of his treasure, I would bring him something that would rid them of their rats. The King gladly gave his word, and I sent one of the

sailors to the ship to fetch Dick's cat. When Tabby was brought in, you should have seen her. The sailor could scarcely hold her, she was so eager to get at those rats. She leaped out of his arms, and in a few minutes had killed all the rats and mice in the room and was busy watching at their holes for any others that might appear. The King was overjoyed. Then I picked Tabby up in my arms and carried her over to the Queen. The Queen was afraid of her at first, but when I showed her how to stroke Tabby's head, the old cat began to purr and rub up against her, and the Queen clapped her hands and said,

" 'This is the most wonderful animal in the world—so ferocious that she kills our rats and so gentle that she allows herself to be held and patted. She is well worth half the treasure. We will pay gladly and keep this animal in comfort as long as she lives.'

"So Tabby remains in Barbary, but in return for her I have brought Mr. Dick Whittington one of the largest fortunes in jewels, silver, and gold that has ever been brought to London."

When the captain had finished speaking, there was silence in the room. Then Mr. Fitzwarren said,

"Come forward, Mr. Dick Whittington," and poor Dick came out of his dark corner to receive his great fortune.

"Now, my boy," continued Mr. Fitzwarren, "I know of no one who deserves his good luck more than you. You are far, far richer than I shall ever be, and I hope with all my heart that you may enjoy your wealth through a long life."

Dick was so overcome he could hardly speak. When he got his voice, he thanked them all and insisted upon giving everyone a handsome present, from the captain to the cook.

After this, Dick bought himself some good clothes and went to school. Years passed, and little Dick Whittington grew to be a fine young man. He had loved Alice Fitzwarren all these years, and so, when he was grown up, they were married, and all the finest people in London came to the wedding.

Mr. Whittington and his lady lived in great splendor, but Dick never forgot the hardships of his early life, and he was always helping the poor. He was sheriff of London and then he was thrice Lord Mayor. He always remembered, as long as he lived, that he owed his great good fortune to the bells of Bow Church and a simple old cat called Tabby.

The Lad Who Went to the North Wind

Retold by GEORGE WEBBE DASENT

ONCE on a time there was an old widow who had one son, and as she was feeble and weak, her son had to go up into the storehouse to fetch meal for cooking. But when he got outside the storehouse and was just going down the steps, there came the North Wind, puffing and blowing, caught up the meal and so away with it through the air. Then the lad went back into the storehouse for more, but when he came out again on the steps, if the North Wind didn't come again and carry off the meal with a puff. And, more than that, he did so a third time. At this the lad got very angry, and as he thought it hard that the North Wind should behave so, he decided to visit him and ask him to give up the meal.

So the lad went. The way was long, and he walked and walked, but at last he came to the North Wind's house.

"Good day," said the lad, "and thank you for coming to see us yesterday."

"GOOD DAY!" answered the North Wind, for his voice was loud and gruff, "And thanks for coming to see me. What do you want?"

"Oh," answered the lad, "I only wished to ask you to be so good as to let me have back that meal you took from me on the storehouse steps, for we haven't much to live on. If you're to go on snapping up the morsel we have, there'll be nothing for it but to starve."

"I haven't got your meal," said the North Wind, "but if you are in such need, I'll give you a cloth which will get you everything you want, if you only say,

" 'Cloth, spread yourself, and serve up all kinds of good dishes!' "

With this the lad was well content. But, as the way was so long that he couldn't get home in one day, he turned into an inn on the way. When suppertime came, he laid the cloth on a table which stood in the corner, and said,

"Cloth, spread yourself, and serve up all kinds of good dishes."

He had scarce said so before the cloth did as it was bid, and all who stood by thought it a fine thing, but most of all the landlord. So, when all were fast asleep, at dead of night, he took the lad's cloth, and put another in its stead, just like the one he had got from the North Wind, but which couldn't so much as serve up dry bread.

So, when the lad woke, he took his cloth and went off with it, and that day he got home to his mother.

"Now," said he, "I've been to the North Wind's house, and a good fellow he is, for he gave me this cloth. When I say to it,

" 'Cloth, spread yourself, and serve up all kinds of good dishes,' I get any sort of food I please."

"All very true, I dare say," said his mother, "but seeing is be-

lieving, and I shan't believe it till I see it."

So the lad made haste, drew out a table, and laid the cloth on it, and said,

"Cloth, spread yourself, and serve up all kinds of good dishes."

But never a bit of dry bread did the cloth serve up.

"Well!" said the lad, "there's no help for it but to go to the North Wind again," and away he went.

So he came to where the North Wind lived, late in the afternoon.

"Good evening!" said the lad.

"Good evening!" said the North Wind.

"I want my rights for that meal of ours which you took," said the lad. "As for that cloth I got, it isn't worth a penny."

"I've got no meal," said the North Wind, "but yonder you have a ram which coins nothing but golden ducats as soon as you say to it,

" 'Ram, ram! Make money!' "

So the lad thought this a fine thing, but as it was too far to get home that day, he turned in for the night to the same inn where he had slept before.

Before he called for anything, he tried the truth of what the North Wind had said of the ram, and found it all right. But when the landlord saw that, he thought it was a famous ram, and when the lad had fallen asleep, he took another which couldn't coin gold ducats, and changed the two.

Next morning off went the lad, and when he got home to his mother, he said,

"After all, the North Wind is a jolly fellow, for now he has given me a ram which can coin golden ducats if I only say,

" 'Ram, ram! Make money!' "

"All very true, I dare say," said his mother, "but I shan't believe any such stuff until I see the ducats made."

"Ram, ram! Make money!" said the lad, but the ram didn't make any money.

So the lad went back again to the North Wind, in desperation, and said the ram was worth nothing, and he must have his rights.

"Well," said the North Wind, "I've nothing else to give you but that old stick in the corner yonder, but if you say,

" 'Stick, stick! Lay on!' it lays on till you give the command, 'Stick, stick! Now stop!' "

So, as the way was long, the lad turned in this night, too, to the landlord. As he could pretty well guess how things stood as to the cloth and the ram, he lay down at once on the bench and began to snore, as if he were asleep.

Now the landlord, who easily saw that the stick must be worth something, hunted up one which was like it, and when he heard the lad snore, was going to change the two. But the lad called,

"Stick, stick! Lay on!"

So the stick began to beat the landlord, till he jumped over chairs, and tables, and benches, and yelled and roared,

"Oh my! Oh my! Bid the stick be still, else it will beat me to death, and you shall have back both your cloth and your ram."

When the lad thought the landlord had got enough, he said,

"Stick, stick! Now stop!"

Then he took his cloth and put it into his pocket, and went home with his stick in his hand, leading the ram by a cord round its horns, and so he got his rights for the meal he had lost.

Tom Tit Tot

Retold by JOSEPH JACOBS

ONCE upon a time there was a woman, and she baked five pies. And when they came out of the oven, they were that overbaked the crusts were too hard to eat. So she said to her daughter,

"Darter," said she, "put you them there pies on the shelf, and leave 'em there a little, and they'll come again." She meant, you know, the crust would get soft.

But the girl, she said to herself, "Well, if they'll come again, I'll eat 'em now." And she set to work and ate 'em all, first and last.

Well, come suppertime the woman said, "Go you, and get one o' them there pies. I dare say they've come again now."

The girl went and she looked, and there was nothing but the dishes. So back she came and said she, "Noo, they ain't come again."

"Not one of 'em?" said the mother.

"Not one of 'em," said she.

"Well, come again, or not come again," said the woman, "I'll have one for supper."

"But you can't, if they ain't come," said the girl.

"But I can," said she. "Go you, and bring the best of 'em."

"Best or worst," said the girl, "I've ate 'em all, and you can't have one till that's come again."

Well, the woman she was done, and she took her spinning to the door to spin, and as she spun she sang:

My darter ha' ate five, five pies today.
My darter ha' ate five, five pies today.

The King was coming down the street, and he heard her sing, but what she sang he couldn't hear, so he stopped and said,

"What was that you were singing, my good woman?"

The woman was ashamed to let him hear what her daughter had been doing, so she sang, instead of that:

My darter ha' spun five, five skeins today.
My darter ha' spun five, five skeins today.

"Stars o' mine!" said the King. "I never heard tell of anyone that could do that."

Then he said, "Look you here, I want a wife, and I'll marry your daughter. But look you here," said he, "eleven months out of the year she shall have all she likes to eat, and all the gowns

she likes to get, and all the company she likes to keep. But the last month of the year she'll have to spin five skeins every day, and if she don't I shall kill her."

"All right," said the woman; for she thought what a grand marriage that was. And as for the five skeins, when the time came, there'd be plenty of ways of getting out of it, and likeliest, he'd have forgotten all about it.

Well, so they were married. And for eleven months the girl had all she liked to eat, and all the gowns she liked to get, and all the company she liked to keep.

But when the time was getting over, she began to think about the skeins and to wonder if he had 'em in mind. But not one word did he say about 'em, and she thought he'd wholly forgotten 'em.

However, the last day of the last month he took her to a room she'd never set eyes on before. There was nothing in it but a spinning wheel and a stool. And, said he, "Now, my dear, here you'll be shut in tomorrow with some victuals and some flax, and if you haven't spun five skeins by the night, your head'll go off."

And away he went about his business.

Well, she was that frightened. She'd always been such a gatless girl that she didn't so much as know how to spin, and what was she to do tomorrow with no one to come nigh her to help her? She sat down on a stool in the kitchen, and, law, how she did cry!

However, all of a sudden she heard a sort of a knocking low down on the door. She upped and oped it, and what should she see but a small little black thing with a long tail. That looked up at her right curious, and that said,

"What are you a-crying for?"

"What's that to you?" said she.

"Never you mind," that said, "but tell me what you're a-crying for."

"That won't do me no good if I do," said she.

"You don't know that," that said, and twirled that's tail round.

"Well," said she, "that won't do no harm, if that don't do no good," and she upped and told about the pies, and the skeins, and everything.

"This is what I'll do," said the little black thing. "I'll come to your window every morning and take the flax and bring it spun at night."

"What's your pay?" said she.

That looked out of the corner of that's eyes, and that said, "I'll give you three guesses every night to guess my name. If you haven't guessed it before the month's up, you shall be mine."

Well, she thought she'd be sure to guess that's name before the month was up. "All right," said she, "I agree."

"All right," that said, and, law, how that twirled that's tail!

Well, the next day, her husband took her into the room, and there was the flax and the day's food.

"Now, there's the flax," said he, "and if that ain't spun up this night, off goes your head." And then he went out and locked the door.

He'd hardly gone, when there was a knocking against the window.

She upped and she oped it, and there sure enough was the little old thing sitting on the ledge.

"Where's the flax?" said he.

"Here it be," said she. And she gave it to him.

Well, come the evening, a knocking came again to the window. She upped and she oped it, and there was the little old thing with five skeins of flax on his arm.

"Here it be," said he, and he gave it to her.

"Now, what's my name?" said he.

"What, is that Bill?" said she.

"Noo, that ain't," said he, and he twirled his tail.

"Is that Ned?" said she.

"Noo, that ain't," said he, and he twirled his tail.

"Well, is that Mark?" said she.

"Noo, that ain't," said he, and he twirled his tail harder, and away he flew.

Well, when her husband came in, there were the five skeins ready for him. "I see I

shan't have to kill you tonight, my dear," said he. "You'll have your food and your flax in the morning," said he, and away he went.

Well, every day the flax and the food were brought, and every day that there little black impet used to come mornings and evenings. And all the day the girl sat trying to think of names to say to it when it came at night. But she never hit on the right one. And as it got towards the end of the month, the impet began to look so maliceful, and that twirled that's tail faster and faster each time she gave a guess.

At last it came to the last day but one. The impet came at night along with the five skeins, and that said,

"What, ain't you got my name yet?"

"Is that Nicodemus?" said she.

"Noo, 't ain't," that said.

"Is that Sammle?" said she.

"Noo, 't ain't," that said.

"A-well, is that Methusalem?" said she.

"Noo, 't ain't that neither," that said.

Then that looked at her with that's eyes like a coal o' fire, and that said, "Woman, there's only tomorrow night, and then you'll be mine!" And away it flew.

Well, she felt that horrid. However, she heard the king coming along the passage. In he came, and when he saw the five skeins, he said, said he:

"Well, my dear," said he. "I don't see but what you'll have your skeins ready tomorrow night as well. As I reckon I shan't have to kill you, I'll have supper in here tonight." So they brought supper, and another stool for him, and down the two sat.

Well, he hadn't eaten but a mouthful or so, when he stopped and began to laugh.

"What is it?" said she.

"A-why," said he, "I was out a-hunting today, and I got away to a place in the wood I'd never seen before. And there was an old chalk pit. And I heard a kind of a sort of humming. So I got off my hobby, and I went right quiet to the pit, and I looked down. Well, what should there be but the funniest little black thing you ever set eyes on? And what was that doing, but that had a little spinning wheel, and that was spinning wonderful fast, and twirling that's tail. And as that spun that sang:

Nimmy nimmy not
My name's Tom Tit Tot.

Well, when the girl heard this, she felt as if she could have jumped out of her skin for joy, but she didn't say a word.

Next day that there little thing looked so maliceful when he came for the flax. And when night came, she heard that knocking against the windowpanes. She oped the window, and that come right in on the ledge. That was grinning from ear to ear, and, oh, that's tail was twirling round so fast.

"What's my name?" that said, as that gave her the skeins.

"Is that Solomon?" she said, pretending to be afeard.

"Noo, 't ain't," that said, and that came farther into the room.

"Well, is that Zebedee?" said she again.

"Noo, 't ain't," said the impet. And then that laughed and twirled that's tail till you couldn't hardly see it.

"Take time, woman," that said. "Next guess, and you're mine." And that stretched out that's black hands at her.

Well, she backed a step or two, and she looked at it, and then she laughed out, and, said she, pointing her finger at it:

Nimmy nimmy not
Your name's Tom Tit Tot.

Well, when that heard her, that gave an awful shriek, and away that flew into the dark, and she never saw it any more.

From *English Fairy Tales*

The Three Wishes

Retold by Joseph Jacobs

ONCE upon a time, and be sure 'twas a long time ago, there lived a poor woodman in a great forest, and every day of his life he went out to fell timber. So one day he started out, and the goodwife filled his wallet and slung his bottle on his back, that he might have meat and drink in the forest. He had marked out a huge oak, which, thought he, would furnish many and many a good plank. And when he was come to it, he took his ax in his hand and swung it round his head as though he were minded to fell the tree at one stroke. But he hadn't given one blow, when what should he hear but the pitifulest entreating, and there stood before him a fairy who prayed and beseeched him to spare the tree. He was dazed, as you may fancy, with wonderment and affright, and he couldn't open his mouth to utter a word. But he found his tongue at last. "Well," said he, "I'll do it."

"You've done better for yourself than you know," answered the fairy, "and to show I'm not ungrateful, I'll grant you your next three wishes, be they what they may." And therewith the fairy was no more to be seen, and the woodman slung his wallet over his shoulder and his bottle at his side, and off he started home.

But the way was long, and the poor man was regularly dazed with the wonderful thing that had befallen him. When he got home, there was nothing in his noodle but the wish to sit down and rest. Maybe, too, 'twas a trick of the fairy's. Who can tell? Anyhow down he sat by the blazing fire, and as he sat he waxed hungry, though it was a long way off suppertime yet.

"Hasn't thou naught for supper, dame?" said he to his wife.

"Nay, not for a couple of hours yet," said she.

"Ah!" groaned the woodman. "I wish I'd a good link of black pudding here before me."

No sooner had he said the word, when *clatter, clatter, rustle, rustle,* what should come down the chimney but a link of the finest black pudding the heart of a man could wish for.

If the woodman stared, the goodwife stared three times as much. "What's all this?" said she.

Then all the morning's work came back to the woodman. He told his tale right out, from beginning to end, and as he told it the goodwife glowered and glowered. When he had made an end of it she burst out, "Thou bee'st but a fool, Jan, and I wish the pudding were at thy nose."

Before you could say, "Jack Robinson," there the woodman

sat and his nose was the longer for a link of black pudding.

He gave a pull but it stuck, and she gave a pull but it stuck. And they both pulled till they had nigh pulled the nose off, but it stuck and stuck.

"What's to be done now?" said he.

" 'Tisn't so very unsightly," said she, looking hard at him.

Then the woodman saw that if he wished, he must need wish in a hurry; and wish he did, that the black pudding might come off his nose. Well, there it lay in a dish on the table, and if the goodman and goodwife didn't ride in a golden coach, or dress in silk and satin, why, they had at least as fine a black pudding for their supper as the heart of man could desire.

From *More English Fairy Tales*

The Emperor's New Clothes

By Hans Christian Andersen

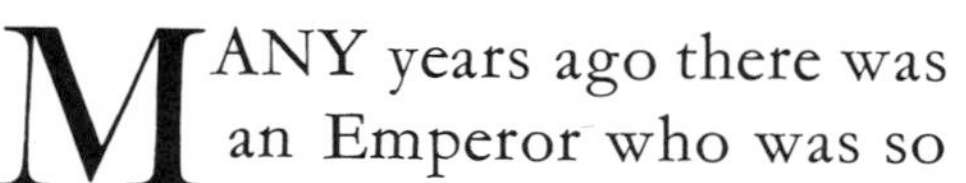

MANY years ago there was an Emperor who was so excessively fond of new clothes that he spent all his money on them. He cared nothing about his soldiers or for the theater, or for driving in the woods, except for the sake of showing off his new clothes. He had a costume for every hour in the day. Instead of saying, as one does about any other King or Emperor, "He is in his council chamber," the people here always said, "The Emperor is in his dressing room."

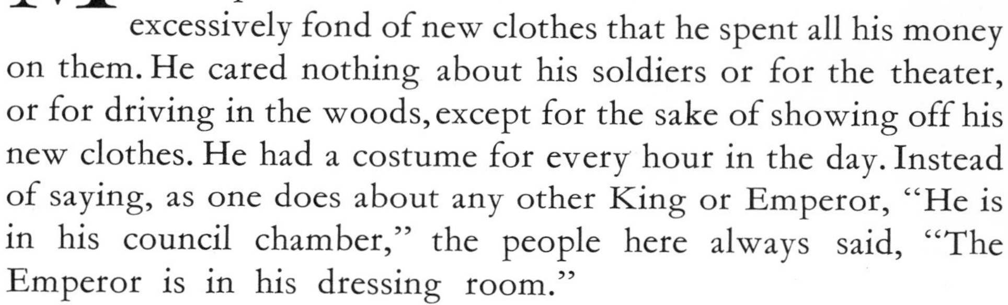

Life was very gay in the great town where he lived. Hosts of strangers came to visit it, and among them one day were two swindlers. They gave themselves out as weavers and said that they knew how to weave the most beautiful fabrics imaginable. Not only were the colors and patterns unusually fine, but the clothes that were made of this cloth had the peculiar quality of becoming invisible to every person who was not fit for the office he held, or who was impossibly dull.

"Those must be splendid clothes," thought the Emperor. "By wearing them I should be able to discover which men in my kingdom are unfitted for their posts. I shall be able to tell the wise men from the fools. Yes, I certainly must order some of that stuff to be woven for me."

The Emperor paid the two swindlers a lot of money in advance, so that they might begin their work at once.

They did put up two looms and pretended to weave, but they had nothing whatever upon their shuttles. At the outset they asked

for a quantity of the finest silk and the purest gold thread, all of which they put into their own bags while they worked away at the empty looms far into the night.

"I should like to know how those weavers are getting on with their cloth," thought the Emperor, but he felt a little queer when he reflected that any one who was stupid or unfit for his post would not be able to see it. He certainly thought that he need have no fears for himself. Still he thought he would send somebody else first to see how the work was getting on. Everybody in the town knew what wonderful power the stuff possessed, and every one was anxious to see how stupid his neighbor was.

"I will send my faithful old minister to the weavers," thought the Emperor. "He will be best able to see how the stuff looks, for he is a clever man and no one fulfills his duties better than he does!"

So the good old minister went into the room where the two swindlers sat working at the empty loom.

"Heaven help us," thought the old minister, opening his eyes very wide. "Why, I can't see a thing!" But he took care not to say so.

Both the swindlers begged him to be good enough to step a little nearer. They asked if he did not think it a good pattern and beautiful coloring, and they pointed to the empty loom. The poor

old minister stared as hard as he could, but he could not see anything, for of course there was nothing to see.

"Good heavens!" thought he. "Is it possible that I am a fool? I have never thought so, and nobody must know it. Am I not fit for my post? It will never do to say that I cannot see the stuff."

"Well, sir, you don't say anything about the stuff," said the one who was pretending to weave.

"Oh, it is beautiful! Quite charming," said the minister, looking through his spectacles. "Such a pattern and such colors! I will certainly tell the Emperor that the stuff pleases me very much."

"We are delighted to hear you say so," said the swindlers, and then they named all the colors and described the peculiar pattern. The old minister paid close attention to what they said, so as to be able to repeat it when he got home to the Emperor.

Then the swindlers went on to demand more money, more silk, and more gold, to be able to proceed with the weaving. They put it all into their own pockets. Not a single strand was ever put into the loom. But they went on as before, pretending to weave at the empty loom.

The Emperor soon sent another faithful official to see how the stuff was getting on and if it would soon be ready. The same thing happened to him as to the minister. He looked and looked, but as there was only the empty loom, he could see nothing at all.

"Is not this a beautiful piece of stuff?" said both the swindlers, showing and explaining the beautiful pattern and colors which were not there to be seen.

"I know I am no fool," thought the man, "so it must be that I am unfit for my good post. It is very strange, but I must not let on." So he praised the stuff he did not see, and assured the swindlers of his delight in the beautiful colors and the originality of the design. "It is absolutely charming!" he said to the Emperor.

Everybody in the town was now talking about this splendid stuff, and the Emperor thought he would like to see it while it was still on the loom. So, accompanied by a number of selected courtiers, among whom were the two faithful officials who had already seen the imaginary stuff, he went to visit the crafty impostors. They were working away as hard as ever they could at the empty loom.

"It is magnificent!" said both the honest officials. "Only see, Your Majesty, what a design! What colors!" And they pointed to the empty loom, for they each thought the others could see the stuff.

"What!" thought the Emperor. "I see nothing at all. This is terrible! Am I a fool? Am I not fit to be Emperor? Why, nothing worse could happen to me!

"Oh, it is beautiful," said the Emperor. "It has my highest approval." He nodded his satisfaction as he gazed at the empty loom. Nothing would induce him to say that he could not see anything.

The whole suite gazed and gazed, but saw nothing more than all the others. However, they all exclaimed with His Majesty, "It is very beautiful!" They advised him to wear a suit made of this wonderful cloth on the occasion of a great procession which was just about to take place. "Magnificent! Gorgeous! Excellent!" went from mouth to mouth. They were all equally delighted with it. The Emperor gave each of the weavers an order of knighthood to be worn in his buttonhole and the title of "Gentleman Weaver."

The swindlers sat up the whole night before the day on which the procession was to take place. They burned sixteen candles, so that people might see how anxious they were to get the Emperor's new clothes ready. They pretended to take the stuff off the loom. They cut it out in the air with a huge pair of scissors, and they stitched away with needles without any thread in them.

At last they said, "Now the Emperor's new clothes are ready."

The Emperor, with his grandest courtiers, went to them himself. Both the swindlers raised one arm in the air, as if they were holding something. They said, "See, these are the trousers. This is the coat. Here is the mantle," and so on. "They are as light as a spider's web. One might think one had nothing on, but that is the very beauty of it."

"Yes," said all the courtiers, but they could not see anything, for there was nothing to see.

"Will Your Imperial Majesty be graciously pleased to take off your clothes?" said the impostors. "Then we may put on the new ones, along here before the great mirror."

The Emperor took off all his clothes, and the impostors pretended to give him one article of dress after the other of the new clothes which they had pretended to make. They pretended to fasten something around his waist and to tie on something. This was the train. The Emperor turned round and round in front of the mirror.

"How well His Majesty looks in the new clothes! How becoming they are!" cried all the people. "What a design, and what colors! They are most gorgeous robes!"

"The canopy is waiting outside which is to be carried over Your Majesty in the procession," said the master of ceremonies.

"Well, I am quite ready," said the Emperor. "Don't the clothes fit well?" Then he turned round again in front of the mirror, so that he should seem to be looking at his grand things.

The chamberlains who were to carry the train stooped and pretended to lift it from the ground with both hands, and they walked along with their hands in the air. They dared not let it appear that they could not see anything.

Then the Emperor walked along in the procession under the gorgeous canopy, and everybody in the streets and at the windows exclaimed, "How beautiful the Emperor's new clothes are! What a splendid train! And they fit to perfection!" Nobody would let it appear that he could see nothing, for that would prove that he was not fit for his post, or else he was a fool. None of the Emperor's clothes had been so successful before.

"But he has nothing on," said a little child.

"Oh, listen to the innocent," said its father. And one person whispered to the other what the child had said. "He has nothing on—a child says he has nothing on!"

"But he has nothing on!" at last cried all the people.

The Emperor writhed, for he knew it was true. But he thought, "The procession must go on now." So he held himself stiffer than ever, and the chamberlains held up the invisible train.

The Fisherman and His Wife

By Jakob and Wilhelm Grimm

THERE was once a fisherman who lived with his wife in a ditch, close by the seaside. The fisherman used to go out all day long a-fishing. One day, as he sat on the shore with his rod, looking at the shining water and watching his line, all of a sudden his float was dragged away deep under the sea, and in drawing it up he pulled a great fish out of the water.

The fish said to him, "Pray let me live. I am not a real fish; I am an enchanted prince. Put me in the water again, and let me go."

"Oh!" said the man. "You need not make so many words about the matter. I wish to have nothing to do with a fish that can talk; so swim away as soon as you please."

He put the fish back into the water, and it darted straight down to the bottom, leaving a long streak of blood behind it.

When the fisherman went home to his wife in the ditch, he told her how he had caught a great fish, and how it had told him it was an enchanted prince, and that on hearing it speak he had let it go again.

"Did you not ask it for anything?" said the wife.

"No," said the man, "what should I ask for?"

"Ah!" said the wife. "We live very wretchedly here in this miserable ditch. Do go back, and tell the fish we want a little cottage."

The fisherman did not much like the business. However, he went to the sea, and when he came there the water looked all yellow and green. And he stood at the water's edge, and said,

> O man of the sea!
> Come listen to me,
> For Alice my wife,
> The plague of my life,
> Hath sent me to beg a boon of thee!

Then the fish came swimming to him, and said, "Well, what does she want?"

"Ah," answered the fisherman, "my wife says that when I had caught you, I ought to have asked you for something before I let you go again. She does not like living any longer in the ditch, and wants a little cottage."

"Go home, then," said the fish. "She is in the cottage already."

So the man went home and

saw his wife standing at the door of a cottage.

"Come in, come in," said she. "Is not this much better than the ditch?"

And there was a parlor, and a bedchamber, and a kitchen, and behind the cottage there was a little garden with all sorts of flowers and fruits, and a courtyard full of ducks and chickens.

"Ah," said the fisherman, "how happily we shall live!"

"We will try to do so, at least," said his wife.

Everything went right for a week or two, and then Dame Alice said, "Husband, there is not room enough in this cottage. The courtyard and garden are a great deal too small. I should like to have a large stone castle to live in. So go to the fish again and tell him to give us a castle."

"Wife," said the fisherman, "I don't like to go to him again, for perhaps he will be angry. We ought to be content with the cottage."

"Nonsense," said the wife, "he will do it very willingly. Go along, and try."

The fisherman went, but his heart was very heavy, and when he came to the sea, it looked blue and gloomy, though it was quite calm, and he went close to it and said,

O man of the sea!
Come listen to me,
For Alice my wife,
The plague of my life,
Hath sent me to beg a boon of thee!

"Well, what does she want now?" said the fish.

"Ah!" said the man very sorrowfully, "my wife wants to live in a stone castle."

"Go home, then," said the fish. "She is standing at the door of it already."

So away went the fisherman and found his wife standing

before a great castle.

"See," said she, "is not this grand?"

With that they went into the castle together and found a great many servants there and the rooms all richly furnished and full of golden chairs and tables. Behind the castle was a garden, and a wood half a mile long, full of sheep, and goats, and hares, and deer; and in the courtyard were stables and cowhouses.

"Well," said the man, "now will we live contented and happy in this beautiful castle for the rest of our lives."

"Perhaps we may," said the wife, "but let us consider and sleep upon it before we make up our minds." So they went to bed.

The next morning when Dame Alice awoke it was broad daylight, and she jogged the fisherman with her elbow and said, "Get up, husband, and bestir yourself, for we must be king of all the land."

"Wife, wife," said the man, "why should we wish to be king?

I will not be king."

"Then I will," said Alice.

"But, wife," answered the fisherman, "how can you be king? The fish cannot make you a king."

"Husband," said she, "say no more about it, but go and try. I will be king!"

So the man went away, quite sorrowful to think that his wife should want to be king. The sea looked sorrowful, too. It was a dark gray color, and was covered with swirling foam as the fisherman cried out,

O man of the sea!
Come listen to me,
For Alice my wife,
The plague of my life,
Hath sent me to beg a boon of thee!

"Well, what would she have now?" said the fish, coming up out of the water.

"Alas!" said the man, "my wife wants to be king."

"Go home," said the fish. "She is king already." And he darted away.

Then the fisherman went home, and as he came close to the palace, he saw a troop of soldiers and heard the sound of drums and trumpets. When he entered, he saw his wife sitting on a high throne of gold and diamonds, with a golden crown upon her head. On each side of her stood six beautiful maidens, each a head taller than the other. Everything about her was magnificent.

"Well, wife," said he, "are you king?"

"Yes," said she, "I am king."

And when he had looked at her for a long time, he said," Ah, wife! What a fine thing it is to be king! Now we shall never have anything more to wish for." And he turned to go out of the room.

"I don't know how that may be," said she. "Never is a long time. I am king, 'tis true, but I begin to be tired of it, and I think I should like to be emperor."

"Alas, wife! Why should you wish to be emperor?" said the fisherman.

"Husband," said she, "go to the fish. I say I will be emperor. You must tell him."

"Ah, wife!" replied the fisherman. "The fish cannot make an emperor, and I should not like to ask for such a thing, truly I should not!"

"I am king," said Alice, sternly, "and you are my slave, so go directly!"

So the fisherman was obliged to go, and he muttered as he went along, "This will come to no good. It is too much to

William Pène Dubois

ask. The fish will be tired at last, and then we shall repent of what we have done."

He soon arrived at the sea, and the water was quite black and muddy, and a mighty whirlwind blew over it, but he went to the shore and said,

O man of the sea!
Come listen to me,
For Alice my wife,
The plague of my life,
Hath sent me to beg a boon of thee!

"What would she have now!" said the fish.

"Ah," said the fisherman, in a sad tone of voice, "she wants to be emperor."

"Go home," said the fish, turning away, "she is emperor already."

So he went home again, and as he came near he saw his wife sitting on a very lofty throne made of solid gold, with a great crown on her head full two yards high. On each side of her stood her guards and attendants in a row, each one smaller than the other, from the tallest giant down to a little dwarf no bigger than my finger. And before her stood princes, and dukes, and earls; and the fisherman went up to her and said,

"Wife, are you emperor?"

"Yes," said she, "I am emperor."

"Ah!" said the man as he gazed upon her, "what a fine thing it is to be emperor!"

"Husband," said she, "why should we stay at being emperor? I will think of something else finer, I am sure." And she began at once to plan.

Then they went to bed, but Dame Alice could not sleep all night for thinking what she should be next. At last morning came, and the sun rose.

"Ha!" thought she, as she looked at it through the window. "Cannot I prevent the sun rising?"

At this she was very angry, and she wakened her husband and said, "Husband, go to the fish and tell him I want to be lord of the sun and moon."

The fisherman was half asleep, but the thought frightened him so much that he started and fell out of bed.

"Alas, wife!" said he. "Cannot you be content to be emperor?"

"No," said she, "I am very uneasy, and cannot bear to see the sun and moon rise without my leave. Go to the fish directly."

Then the man went, trembling with fear, and as he was going down to the shore a dreadful storm arose, so that the trees and the rocks shook. The heavens became black, and the lightning played, and the thunder rolled; and you might have seen in the sea great black waves like mountains with a white crown of foam upon them; and the fisherman said,

O man of the sea!
Come listen to me,
For Alice my wife,
The plague of my life,
Hath sent me to beg a boon of thee!

"What does she want now?" said the fish.

"Ah!" said he, "she wants to be lord of the sun and moon."

"Go home," said the fish, "to your ditch again!"

And there they live to this day.

Prince Wicked and the Grateful Animals

Retold by Ellen C. Babbitt

ONCE upon a time a King had a son named Prince Wicked. He was fierce and cruel, and he spoke to nobody without abuse, or blows. Like grit in the eye, was Prince Wicked to every one, both in the palace and out of it.

His people said to one another, "If he acts this way while he is a prince, how will he act when he is king?"

One day when the Prince was swimming in the river, suddenly a great storm came on, and it grew very dark.

In the darkness the servants who were with the Prince swam from him, saying to themselves, "Let us leave him alone in the river, and he may drown."

When they reached the shore, some of the servants who had not gone into the river said, "Where is Prince Wicked?"

"Isn't he here?" they asked. "Perhaps he came out of the river in the darkness and went home." Then the servants all went back to the palace.

The King asked where his son was, and again the servants said, "Isn't he here, O King? A great storm came on soon after we went into the water. It grew very dark. When we came out of the water, the Prince was not with us."

At once the King had the gates thrown open. He and all his men searched up and down the banks of the river for the missing prince. But no trace of him could be found.

In the darkness the Prince had been swept down the river. He was crying for fear he would drown, when he came across a log. He climbed upon the log, and floated farther down the river.

When the great storm arose, the water rushed into the homes of a Rat and a Snake who lived on the river bank. The Rat and the Snake swam out into the river and found the same log the Prince had found. The Snake climbed upon one end of the log, and the Rat climbed upon the other.

On the river's bank a cottonwood tree grew, and a young Parrot lived in its branches. The storm pulled up this tree, and it fell into the river. The heavy rain beat down the Parrot when it tried to fly, and it could not go far. Looking down it saw the log, and flew down to rest. Now there were four on the log floating downstream together.

Just around the bend in the river a certain poor man had built himself a hut. As he walked to and fro late at night listening to the storm, he heard the loud cries of the Prince. The poor man said to himself, "I must get that man out of the water. I must save his life." So he shouted, "I will save you! I will save you!" as he swam out in the river.

Soon he reached the log. Pushing it by one end, he soon pushed it into the bank. The Prince jumped up and down, he was so glad to be safe and sound on dry land.

Then the poor man saw the Snake, the Rat, and the Parrot, and carried them to his hut. He built a fire, putting the animals near it so they could get dry. He took care of them first, because they were weaker, and afterwards he looked after the comfort of the Prince.

Then the poor man brought food and set it before them,

looking after the animals first and the Prince afterwards. This made the young prince angry, and he said to himself, "This poor man does not treat me like a prince. He takes care of the animals before taking care of me." Then the Prince began to hate the poor man.

A few days later, when the Prince, and the Snake, the Rat, and the Parrot were rested, and the storm was all over, the Snake said good-by to the poor man with these words: "Father, you have been very kind to me. I know where there is some buried gold. If ever you want gold, you shall have only to come to my home and call, 'Snake!' and I will show you the buried gold. It shall all be yours."

Next the Rat said good-by to the poor man. "If ever you want money," said the Rat, "come to my home, and call out, 'Rat!' and I will show you where a great deal of money is buried near my home. It shall all be yours."

Then the Parrot came, saying, "Father, silver and gold have I none. But if you ever want choice rice, come to where I live and call, 'Parrot!' and I will call all my family and friends together, and we will gather the choicest rice in the fields for you."

Last came the Prince. In his heart he hated the poor man who had saved his life. But he pretended to be as thankful as the animals had been, saying, "Come to me when I am King, and I will give you great riches." So saying, he went away.

Not long after this the Prince's father died, and Prince Wicked was made King. He was then very rich.

By and by the poor man said to himself, "Each of the four whose lives I saved made a promise to me. I will see if they will keep their promises."

First of all he went to the Snake, and standing near his hole, the poor man called out, "Snake!"

At once the Snake darted forth, and with every mark of re-

spect he said, "Father, in this place there is much gold. Dig it up and take it all."

"Very well," said the poor man. "When I need it, I will not forget."

After visiting for a while, the poor man said good-by to the Snake, and went to where the Rat lived, calling out, "Rat!"

The Rat came at once, and did as the Snake had done, showing the poor man where the money was buried.

"When I need it, I will come for it," said the poor man.

Going next to the Parrot, he called out, "Parrot!" and the

bird flew down from the treetops as soon as he heard the call.

"O Father," said the Parrot, "shall I call together all my family and friends to gather choice rice for you?"

The poor man, seeing that the Parrot was willing and ready to keep his promise, said, "I do not need rice now. If ever I do, I will not forget your offer."

Last of all, the poor man went into the city where the King lived. The King, seated on his great white elephant, was riding through the city. The King saw the poor man, and said to himself, "That poor man has come to ask me for the great riches I promised to give him. I must have his head cut off before he can tell the people how he saved my life when I was the Prince."

So the King called his servants to him and said, "You see that poor man over there? Seize him and bind him. Beat him at every corner of the street as you march him out of the city, and then chop off his head."

The servants had to obey their King. So they seized and bound the poor man. They beat him at every corner of the street. The poor man did not cry out, but he said, over and over again, "It is better to save poor, weak animals than to save a Prince."

At last some wise men among the crowds along the street asked the poor man what Prince he had saved. Then the poor man told the whole story, ending with the words, "By saving your King, I brought all this pain upon myself."

The wise men and all the rest of the crowd cried out, "This poor man saved the life of our King, and now the King has ordered him to be killed. How can we be sure that he will not have any, or all, of us killed? Let us kill him." And in their anger they rushed from every side upon the King as he rode on his elephant, and with arrows and stones they killed him then and there.

Then they made the poor man King to rule over them.

The poor man ruled his people well. One day he decided once more to try the Snake, the Rat, and the Parrot. So, followed by many servants, the King went to where the Snake lived.

At the call of "Snake!" out came the Snake from his hole, saying, "Here, O King, is your treasure; take it."

"I will," said the King. "And I want you to come with me."

Then the King had his servants dig up the gold.

Going to where the Rat lived, the King called, "Rat!" Out came the Rat, and said, "Take all the money buried here."

"I will," said the King, and he asked the Rat to go with him.

AND THE GRATEFUL ANIMALS

Then the King went to where the Parrot lived and called, "Parrot!" The Parrot said, "O King, shall I and my family and friends gather rice for you?"

"Not now, not until rice is needed," said the King. "Will you come with us?"

So with the gold, and the money, and with the Snake, the Rat, and the Parrot as well, the King went back to the city.

The King had the gold and the money hidden away in the palace. He had a tube of gold made for the Snake to live in. He had a glass box made for the Rat, and a cage of gold for the Parrot. Each had the food he liked best of all to eat every day, so they lived happily all their lives.

From *More Jataka Tales*

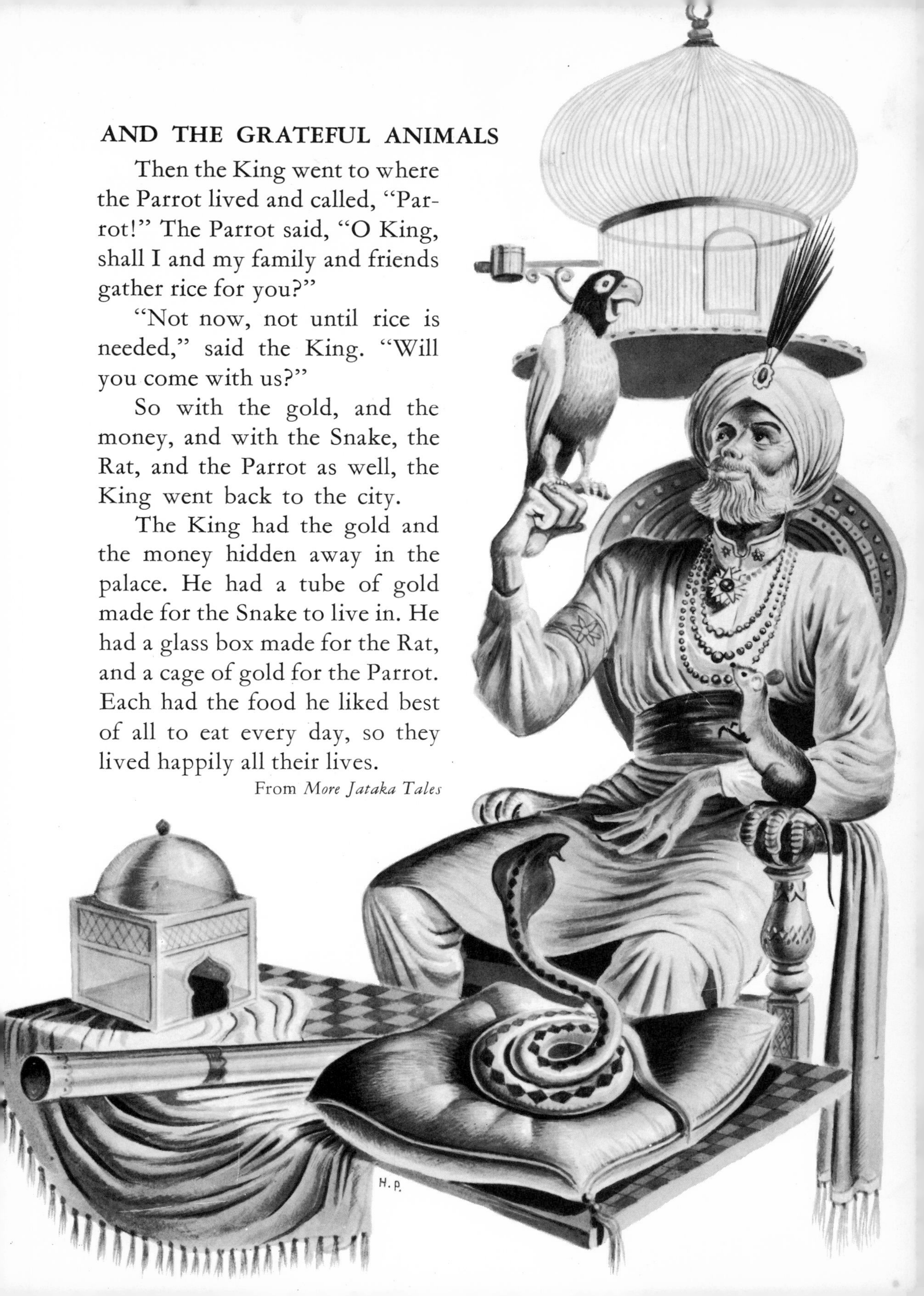

The Real Princess

By Hans Christian Andersen

THERE was once a Prince who wanted to marry a Princess, but she was to be a *real* Princess. So he traveled about, all through the world, to find a real one, but everywhere there was something in the way. There were Princesses enough, but whether they were *real* Princesses he could not quite make out. There was always something that did not seem quite right. So he came home again, and was quite sad, for he wished so much to have a real Princess.

One evening a terrible storm came on. It lightened and thundered, the rain streamed down; it was quite fearful! Then there was a knock at the town gate, and the old King went to open it.

It was a Princess who stood outside the gate. But, mercy, how she looked from the rain and the rough weather! The water ran down from her hair and her clothes; it ran in at the points of her shoes and out at the heels; yet she declared she was a real Princess.

"Yes, we shall soon find that out," thought the old Queen. But she said nothing, only went into the bedchamber, took all the bedding off, and put a pea on the flooring of the bedstead. Then she took twenty mattresses and laid them upon the pea, and then twenty eider-down beds upon the mattresses. On this the Princess had to lie all night. In the morning she was asked how she had slept.

"Oh, miserably!" said the Princess. "I scarcely closed my eyes all night long. Goodness knows what was in my bed. I lay upon something hard, so that I am black and blue all over. It is quite dreadful!"

Now they saw that she was a real Princess, for through the twenty mattresses and the twenty eider-down beds she had felt the pea. No one but a real Princess could be so delicate.

So the Prince took her for his wife, for now he knew that he had a true Princess, and the pea was put in the museum, and it is there now unless somebody has carried it off.

Look you, this is a true story.

The Steadfast Tin Soldier

By Hans Christian Andersen

ONCE upon a time there were five-and-twenty tin soldiers. They were all brothers, for they were born of the same old tin spoon. They shouldered arms and looked straight in front of them in their fascinating red and blue uniforms. The very first thing they heard in this world, when the lid was taken off their box, was, "Tin soldiers!" A little boy shouted it, and clapped his hands. The soldiers were a present, for it was his birthday, and now he was busy setting them up. Each soldier was the living image of the others, but there was one who was a little bit different. He had only one leg, for he was the last to be cast and the tin had run out. Still, there he stood, just as steadfast on his one leg as the others on their two; and he is the tin soldier we are going to hear about.

On the table where the soldiers had been set up stood a great many other toys. But the thing that caught the eye more than anything else was a wonderful paper castle, with little windows through which you could see straight in to the halls. In front of the castle there were little trees round a tiny looking glass that was supposed to be a lake. Swans made of wax swam on it, and were mirrored in the glass. This was all very pretty, but the prettiest was a little lady who stood in the open doorway of the castle. She, too, was cut out of paper, but she had on a skirt of the very finest lawn, and a little nar-

row blue ribbon over her shoulder like a scarf. In the middle of it was placed a glittering spangle as big as the whole of her tiny face. The little lady held both her arms outstretched —for she was a dancer—and also lifted one of her legs so high that the tin soldier couldn't see it at all, and thought she had only one leg like himself.

"That's the wife for me," he thought, "but she's a very grand lady. She lives in a castle, and I've only got a box, and there are five-and-twenty of us to share it. It's no place for her. All the same, I must get to know her." And then he laid himself down full length behind a snuff box standing on the table. From there he could watch the graceful little lady who kept standing on one leg without losing her balance.

When it was getting late, all the other tin soldiers were put into their box, and the people in the house went to bed. Then the toys began to play, and they played at receiving visitors, at having wars, and giving balls. The tin soldiers rattled in their box, for they wanted to take part in the fun, but they could not get the lid off. The nutcrackers turned somersaults, and the slate pencil capered about on the slate. Finally there was so much noise that the canary woke up and began to talk—and that in verse, if you please! The only two who did not stir were the tin soldier and the little dancer. She stood firm on the tip of her toe with both arms outstretched. He stood just as steadfast on his one leg, and never took his eyes off her for a moment.

Then the clock struck twelve, and—pop!—up sprang the lid of the snuff box; but there was no snuff in it. No, there was a little black imp—you see it was a trick box.

"Tin soldier," said the imp, "kindly keep your eyes to yourself."

But the tin soldier pretended not to hear.

"Just you wait till tomorrow," said the imp.

Well, when tomorrow came and the children got up, the tin soldier was put on the window sill. And all of a sudden—it was either due to the imp or to the draught—the window flew open, and the soldier fell headfirst out from the third story. It was a hair-raising fall. He found himself standing on his cap, with his bayonet buried between the paving stones, and his one leg pointing straight up in the air.

The servant and the little boy rushed down immediately to look for him. Though they almost stepped on him, they never saw him. If the soldier had shouted, "Here I am!" they would certainly have found him, but he thought it beneath his dignity to shout when he was in uniform.

Then it began to rain. The drops followed each other faster and faster, until it became a regular downpour. When it was all over, two urchins came along.

"Crikey!" said one of them. "Here's a tin soldier! Let's send him sailing!"

So they made a boat out of a newspaper, placed the tin soldier right in the middle of it, and off he sailed down the gutter. The two boys ran along beside him, clapping their hands. Did you ever see waves like that in the gutter—and did you ever see such a strong current? Now don't forget that it had been raining cats and dogs. The paper boat danced up and down, and sometimes whirled round so rapidly that the tin soldier was shaken from head to foot. But he remained steadfast, never blinked an eyelash, looked straight ahead, and kept on shouldering arms.

Suddenly the boat sailed under a long plank covering the gutter. It was as dark there as if he had been in his box.

"I wonder where I can be going?" he thought. "I bet it's the imp wanting to get even with me! Oh, if only the little lady were here with me in the boat, it could be twice as dark for all I'd care!"

At that very moment there appeared a great water rat who lived under the plank.

"Got your passport?" asked the rat. "Haul it out!"

The tin soldier said nothing, but held his rifle tighter than ever. The boat rushed on and the rat after it, gnashing his teeth horribly, and calling out to sticks and straws, "Stop him! Stop him! He hasn't paid any toll! He hasn't shown his passport."

But the current became stronger and stronger. The tin soldier could already catch a glimpse of daylight where the plank ended, but he also heard a roaring noise which might very well have frightened the bravest man. Just imagine! At the end of the plank the water rushed out into a huge canal. The situation was as dangerous for him as shooting a great waterfall would be for us.

By now he had got so near the place that he could not possibly stop. The boat darted out, and the poor tin soldier held himself as stiffly as he could — no one should say of him that he even blinked an eye. The boat whirled round three or four times and filled with water to the very brim; it was bound to sink. The tin soldier was already up to his neck in water. The boat sank deeper and deeper, the paper grew softer and softer. The water now closed over the soldier's head. Then he thought of the pretty little dancer whom he would never see again, and in his ears rang the old song:

Here comes a candle to light you to bed,
Here comes a chopper to chop off your head.

Then the paper fell to pieces, and the tin soldier went right through, and was immediately swallowed by a great fish!

Heavens! How dark it was inside—worse than under the plank! And besides it was terribly cramped, but the tin soldier was as steadfast as ever, and lay there full length with shouldered arms.

The fish bounced about, making the most awful contortions, and finally lay absolutely still. Something like a streak of lightning flashed through it, broad daylight appeared, and a voice was heard exclaiming, "Look who's here!" The fish had been caught, taken to market and sold, and had now landed in the kitchen where the cook cut it open with a knife.

She seized the soldier by his middle and carried him into the sitting room, where everybody wanted to see so remarkable a fellow who had traveled about in the inside of a fish. But the tin soldier was not at all proud of it. He was placed on the table, and there—now, isn't that the most extraordinary coincidence?—the tin soldier found himself in the very same room he had been in before! He saw the very same children and the very same toys on the table. The beautiful castle with the pretty little dancer was still there.

THE STEADFAST TIN SOLDIER

She was still balancing herself on one leg, and lifting the other high up. She, too, was steadfast! That moved the tin soldier; he almost wept tin tears—only that isn't done in uniform. He looked at her and she looked at him, but they said nothing.

At that very moment one of the little boys picked up the soldier and threw him into the stove. There was no reason why he should have done that. It was undoubtedly the imp in the snuff box who was to blame for it.

The tin soldier stood all lit up, and felt a heat that was terrible, but whether it came from the real fire or from love, he did not know. He had lost all his bright colors; but whether that had happened on his voyage, or had been caused by sorrow, nobody could tell. He looked at the little lady, she looked at him, and he felt that he was melting, but still he stood steadfast with shouldered arms. Then suddenly a door opened, the wind caught the dancer, and she flew, like a sylph, into the stove to the tin soldier, blazed up in a flame, and was gone. The tin soldier melted down into a lump, and when next day the servant took out the ashes, she found him in the shape of a little tin heart. But of the dancer nothing remained except the spangle, and that was burnt as black as coal.

From *It's Perfectly True*, translated by Paul Leyssac

Talk

By Harold Courlander and George Herzog

ONCE, not far from the city of Accra on the Gulf of Guinea, a country man went out to his garden to dig up some yams to take to market. While he was digging, one of the yams said to him,

"Well, at last you're here. You never weeded me, but now you come around with your digging stick. Go away and leave me alone!"

The farmer turned around and looked at his cow in amazement. The cow was chewing her cud and looking at him.

"Did you say something?" he asked.

The cow kept on chewing and said nothing, but the man's dog spoke up.

"It wasn't the cow who spoke to you," the dog said. "It was the yam. The yam says leave him alone."

The man became angry, because his dog had never talked before, and he didn't like his tone besides. So he took his knife and cut a branch from a palm tree to whip his dog. Just then the palm tree said,

"Put that branch down!"

The man was getting very upset about the way things were

going, and he started to throw the palm branch away, but the palm branch said,

"Man, put me down softly!"

He put the branch down gently on a stone, and the stone said,

"Hey, take that thing off me!"

This was enough, and the frightened farmer started to run for his village. On the way he met a fisherman going the other way with a fish trap on his head.

"What's the hurry?" the fisherman asked.

"My yam said, 'Leave me alone!' Then the dog said, 'Listen to what the yam says!' When I went to whip the dog with a palm branch the tree said, 'Put that branch down!' Then the palm branch said, 'Do it softly!' Then the stone said, 'Take that thing off me!' "

"Is that all?" the man with the fish trap asked. "Is that so frightening?"

"Well," the man's fish trap said, "did he take it off the stone?"

"Wah!" the fisherman shouted. He threw the fish trap on the ground and began to run with the farmer, and on the trail they met a weaver with a bundle of cloth on his head.

"Where are you going in such a rush?" he asked them.

"My yam said, 'Leave me alone!' " the farmer said. "The dog said, 'Listen to what the yam says!' The tree said, 'Put that branch down!' The branch said, 'Do it softly!' And the stone said, 'Take that thing off me!' "

"And then," the fisherman continued, "the fish trap said, 'Did he take it off?' "

"That's nothing to get excited about," the weaver said, "no reason at all."

"Oh, yes, it is," his bundle of cloth said. "If it happened to you, you'd run too!"

"Wah!" the weaver shouted. He threw his bundle on the trail and started running with the other men.

They came panting to the ford in the river and found a man bathing.

"Are you chasing a gazelle?" he asked them.

The first man said breathlessly,

"My yam talked to me, and it said, 'Leave me alone!' And my dog said, 'Listen to your yam!' And when I cut myself a branch the tree said, 'Put that branch down!' And the branch said, 'Do it softly!' And the stone said, 'Take that thing off me!' "

The fisherman panted,

"And my trap said, 'Did he?' "

The weaver wheezed,

"And my bundle of cloth said, 'You'd run, too!' "

"Is that why you're running?" the man in the river asked.

"Well, wouldn't you run if you were in their position?" the river said.

The man jumped out of the water and began to run with the

others. They ran down the main street of the village to the house of the Chief. The Chief's servants brought his stool out, and he came and sat on it to listen to their complaints. The men began to recite their troubles.

"I went out to my garden to dig yams," the farmer said, waving his arms. "Then everything began to talk! My yam said, 'Leave me alone!' My dog said, 'Pay attention to your yam!' The tree said, 'Put that branch down!' The branch said, 'Do it softly!' And the stone said, 'Take it off me!' "

"And my fish trap said, 'Well, did he take it off?' " the fisherman said.

"And my cloth said, 'You'd run, too!' " the weaver said.

"And the river said the same," the bather said hoarsely, his eyes bulging.

The Chief listened to them patiently, but he couldn't refrain from scowling.

"Now this is really a wild story," he said at last. "You'd better all go back to your work before I punish you for disturbing the peace."

So the men went away, and the Chief shook his head and mumbled to himself, "Nonsense like that upsets the community."

"Fantastic, isn't it?" his stool said. "Imagine, a talking yam!"

From *The Cow-Tail Switch*

*The Clever Old Woman of Carcassonne**

By Simone Chamoud

ONCE, long ago, when the town of Carcassonne was in siege, the inhabitants had nothing left to eat. Hunger and sickness had killed so many people that those who were still alive were in despair.

The Mayor of the town assembled all the people on the public square, to speak to them. "My friends," he said, "we shall have to surrender to the enemy. Our provisions are all gone."

"No, no!" cried a shabby little old woman. "Don't give up yet. I am sure that the enemy will leave soon. If you will do as I tell you, I promise that the town will be saved."

The Mayor thought it would do no harm to listen to her; and the old woman said, "First of all, bring me a cow."

*Reprinted by permission of the publishers from *Picture Tales from the French* by Simone Chamoud, copyright 1933, by J. B. Lippincott Company.

"A cow!" the Mayor cried. "Why, there is not one cow left in the whole town. They have all been eaten long ago."

But the old woman insisted that she must have a cow, and every house was searched until at last one was found in the hut of an old miser. He had hidden the animal in the hope of selling it for a goodly sum. But the soldiers seized the cow, in spite of all his wailing.

"Now," ordered the old woman, "bring me a bushel of meal."

"But there is no meal left in the town," the Mayor protested. The old woman insisted, however, that without a bushel of meal she could do nothing. So again soldiers were sent from house to house, to collect every grain they could find, until at length a basketful was brought to the old woman.

After watering the meal to make it heavier, she fed it to the cow. The Mayor declared that it was wicked to give good grain to an animal while women and children were starving, but the old woman only shook her head and smiled knowingly.

Night had fallen before the cow had finished eating, and the old woman led it to the town gates.

"Open the gate," she ordered the sentry; and, as the big iron doors swung open, she quickly pushed the cow through. The enemy soldiers had heard the creaking of the doors, and they came running up to the gate. Great was their joy when they found the cow, and they lost no time in driving it before them to their camp.

"Where did you find this cow?" asked the enemy King.

"Just outside the gates of the town. They must have let it out to graze."

"Oh," exclaimed the King, "I thought they were starving in there! But I must be mistaken, for if they were hungry they would certainly have eaten this cow—even though it is not very plump."

"Yes, they must have more provisions than we thought they had," answered the soldiers. "It's been a long time since *we* have

eaten fresh meat," they said.

"Well," suggested their King, "kill the cow and we shall have steak for dinner."

To their amazement, when the cow was cut open, they found its stomach filled with grain.

When the King heard of this, he said, "If the people of Carcassonne still have enough grain to feed it to their animals, we shall have to wait here too long a time before they surrender. And we ourselves shall probably starve before they do." So he gave orders to break camp, and left with his army that very night.

And that was how Carcassonne became free again. The people carried the old woman in triumph through the streets, and gave her money to live in comfort for the rest of her life.

From *Picture Tales from the French*

*The Flea**

By Ruth Sawyer

ONCE there was and was not a King of Spain. He loved to laugh; he loved a good joke as well as any common fellow. Best of all, he loved a riddle.

One day he was being dressed by his chamberlain. As the royal doublet was being slipped over the royal head, a flea jumped from the safe hiding-place of the stiff lace ruff. He landed directly upon the King.

Quicker than half a wink the King clapped his hand over the flea and began to laugh. "*Por Dios,* a flea! Who ever heard of a King of Spain having a flea? It is monstrous—it is delicious! We must not treat her lightly, this flea. You perceive, my Lord Chamberlain, that having jumped on the royal person, she has now become a royal flea. Consider what we shall do with her."

But the chamberlain was a man of little wit. He could clothe the King's body, but he could

*Reprinted by permission of the publishers from *Picture Tales from Spain* by Ruth Sawyer, copyright 1936, by J. B. Lippincott Company.

not add one ribbon or one button to the King's imagination. "I have it!" said the King at last, exploding again into laughter. "We will pasture out this flea in a great cage—large enough for a goat—an ox—an elephant. She shall be fed enormously. When she is of a proper size I will have her killed and her skin made into a tambourine. The Infanta, my daughter, shall dance to it. We will make a fine riddle out of it. Whichever suitor that comes courting her who can answer the riddle shall marry with her. *There* is a royal joke worthy of a King! Eh, my Lord Chamberlain? And we shall call the flea *Felipa.*"

In his secret heart the chamberlain thought the King quite mad; but all he answered was: "Very good, Your Majesty," and went out to see that proper pasturage was provided for Felipa.

At the end of a fortnight the flea was as large as a rat. At the end of a month she was as large as a cat who might have eaten that rat. At the end of a second month she was the size of a dog who might have chased that cat. At the end of three months she was the size of a calf.

The King ordered Felipa killed. The skin was stretched, dried, beaten until it was as soft, as fine, as silk. Then it was made into a tambourine, with brass clappers and ribbons—the finest tambourine in all Spain.

The Infanta, whose name was Isabel, but who was called Belita for convenience, learned to dance with Felipa very prettily; and the King himself composed a rhyme to go with the riddle. Whenever a suitor came courting, the Infanta would dance and when she had finished, the King would recite:

Belita—Felipa—they dance well together—
Belita—Felipa; now answer me whether
You know this Felipa—this *animalita*.
If you answer right, then you marry Belita.

Princes and dukes came from Spain and Portugal, France

and Italy. They were not dull-witted like the chamberlain and they saw through the joke. The King was riddling about the tambourine. It was made from parchment and they knew perfectly well where parchment came from. So a prince would answer, "A goat, Your Majesty." And a duke would answer, "A sheep, Your Majesty"— each sure he was right. And the Infanta would run away laughing and the King would roar with delight and shout, "Wrong again!"

But after a while the King got tired of this sheep and goat business. He wanted the riddle guessed; he wanted the Infanta married. So he sent forth a command that the next suitor who failed to guess the riddle should be hanged—and short work made of it, too.

That put a stop to the princes and dukes. But far up in the Castilian highlands a shepherd heard about it. He was young, but not very clever. He thought it would be a fine thing for a shepherd to marry an Infanta, so he said to his younger brother, "Manuelito, you shall mind the sheep and goats; I will go to the King's palace."

But his mother said, "Son, you are a *tonto*. How should you guess a riddle when you cannot read or write, and those who can have failed? Stay at home and save yourself a hanging."

Having once made up his mind, nothing would stop him—not even fear. So his mother baked him a *tortilla* to carry with him, gave him her blessing, and let him go.

He hadn't gone far when he was stopped by a little black ant. "Señor Pastor," she cried, "give me a ride to the King's court in your pocket."

"La Hormiguita, you cannot ride in my pocket. There is a *tortilla* there which I shall have for my breakfast. Your feet are dirty from walking, and you will tramp all over it."

"See, I will dust off my feet on the grass here and promise

not to step once on the *tortilla.*"

So the shepherd put the ant into his shepherd pouch and tramped on. Soon he encountered a black beetle who said, "Señor Pastor, give me a ride to the King's court in your pocket."

"El Escarabajo, you cannot ride in my pouch. There is a *tortilla* there which I shall presently have for my breakfast—and who wants a black beetle tramping all over his breakfast!"

"I will fasten my claws into the side of your pouch and not go near the *tortilla.*"

So the shepherd took up the beetle and carried him along. He hadn't gone far when he came up with a little gray mouse who cried, "Señor Pastor, give me a ride to the King's court in your pouch."

But the shepherd shook his head. "Ratonperez, you are too clumsy and I don't like the flavor of your breath. It will spoil my *tortilla* that I intend to have for my breakfast."

"Why not eat the *tortilla* now, and then the breakfast will be over and done with?" And Ratonperez said it so gently, so coaxingly, that the shepherd thought it was a splendid idea. He sat down and ate it. He gave a little crumb to La Hormiguita, a crumb to El Escarabajo, and a big crumb to Ratonperez. Then he went on his road to the King's court, carrying the three creatures with him in his pouch.

When he reached the King's palace he was frightened, frightened. He sat under a cork tree to wait for his courage to grow.

"What are you waiting for?" called the ant, the beetle, and Ratonperez all together.

"I go to answer a riddle. If I fail I shall be hanged. That isn't so pleasant. So I wait where I can enjoy being alive for a little moment longer."

"What is the riddle?"

"I have heard that it has to do with something called Felipa that dances, whoever she may be."

"Go on and we will help you. Hurry, hurry, it is hot in here."

So the shepherd climbed the palace steps, asked for the King, and said that he had come to answer the riddle.

The guard passed him on to the footman, saying, *"Pobrecito!"*

The footman passed him on to the lackey, saying, *"Pobrecito!"*

The lackey passed him on to the court chamberlain, saying, *"Pobrecito!!"* And it was his business to present him to the King.

The King shook his head when he saw the shepherd's staff in his hand and the shepherd's pouch hanging from his belt, and he said, "A shepherd's life is better than no life at all. Better go back to your flocks."

But the shepherd was as rich in stubbornness as he was poor in learning. He insisted he must answer the riddle. So the Infanta came and danced with the tambourine and the King said:

Belita—Felipa—they dance well together—
Belita—Felipa; now answer me whether
You know this Felipa—this *animalita*.
If you answer right, then you marry Belita.

The shepherd strode over and took the tambourine from the hand of the Infanta. He felt the skin carefully, carefully. To himself he said, "I know sheep and I know goats; and it isn't either."

"Can't you guess?" whispered the black beetle from his pouch.

"No," said the shepherd.

"Let me out," said the little ant. "Perhaps I can tell you what it is." So the shepherd unfastened the pouch and La Hormiguita crawled out, unseen by the court. She crawled all over the tambourine and came back whispering, "You can't fool me. I'd know a flea anywhere, any size."

"Don't take all day," shouted the King. "Who is Felipa?"

"She's a flea," said the shepherd.

Then the court was in a flutter.

"I don't want to marry a shepherd," said the Infanta.

"You shan't," said the King.

"I'm the one to say, 'shan't!' " said the shepherd.

"I will grant you any other favor," said the Infanta.

"I will grant you another," said the King.

"It was a long journey here, walking," said the shepherd. "I would like a cart to ride home in."

"And two oxen to draw it," whispered the black beetle.

"And two oxen to draw it," repeated the shepherd.

"You shall have them," said the King.

"And what shall I give you?" asked the Infanta.

"Tell her you want your pouch filled with gold," whispered Ratonperez.

"That's little enough," said the Infanta.

But while the royal groom was fetching the cart and oxen; and the lord of the exchequer was fetching a bag of gold; Ratonperez was gnawing a hole in the pouch. When they came to pour in the gold, it fell through as fast as water, so that all around the feet of the shepherd it rose like a shining yellow stream.

"That's a lot of gold," said the King at last.

"It's enough," said the shepherd. He took his cart, filled it with the gold, drove back to the highlands of Castile. He married a shepherd's daughter, who never had to do anything but sit in a rocking chair and fan herself all day. And that's a contented life, you might say—for anyone who likes it.

From *Picture Tales from Spain*

Salt

By Arthur Ransome

ONCE upon a time there were three brothers, and their father was a great merchant who sent his ships far over the sea, and traded here and there. Well, the names of the two eldest brothers do not matter, but the youngest was called Ivan the Ninny, because he was always playing and never working. If there was a silly thing to do, why, off he went and did it. And so, when the brothers grew up, the father sent the two elder ones off, each in a fine ship laden with gold and jewels, and rings and bracelets, and laces and silks, and sticks with little bits of silver hammered into their handles, and spoons with patterns of blue and red, and everything else you can think of that costs too much to buy. But he made Ivan the Ninny stay at home, and did not give him a ship at all. Ivan saw his brothers go sailing off over the sea on a summer morning, to make their fortunes and come back rich men; and then, for the first time in his life, he wanted to work and do something useful. He went to his father and kissed his hand, and he kissed the hand of his little old mother, and he begged his father to give him a ship so that he could try his fortune like his brothers.

"But you have never done a wise thing in your life, and no one could count all the silly things you've done if he spent a hundred days in counting," said his father.

"True," said Ivan; "but now I am going to be wise, and sail the sea and come back with something in my pockets to show that I am not a ninny any longer. Give me just a little ship, Father mine—just a little ship for myself."

"Give him a little ship," said the mother. "He may not be a ninny after all."

"Very well," said his father. "I will give him a little ship; but I am not going to waste good rubles (silver coins) by giving him a rich cargo."

"Give me any cargo you like," said Ivan.

So his father gave him a little ship, a little old ship, and a cargo of rags and scraps and things that were not fit for anything but to be thrown away. And he gave him a crew of ancient old sailormen who were past work; and Ivan went on board and sailed away at sunset, like the ninny he was. And the feeble, ancient, old sailormen pulled up the ragged, dirty sails; and away they went over the sea to learn what fortune, good or bad, God had in mind for a crew of old men with a ninny for a master.

The fourth day after they set sail, there came a great wind over the sea. The feeble old men did the best they could with the ship; but the old, torn sails tore from the masts, and the wind did what it pleased, and threw the little ship on an unknown island away in the middle of the sea. Then the wind dropped, and left the little ship on the beach, and Ivan the Ninny and his ancient old men, like good Russians, praising God that they were still alive.

"Well, children," said Ivan, for he knew how to talk to sailors, "do you stay here and mend the sails. Make new ones out of the rags we carry as cargo, while I go inland and see if there is anything that could be of use to us."

So the ancient old sailormen sat on deck with their legs crossed, and made sails out of rags, of torn scraps of old brocades, of soiled embroidered shawls, of all the rubbish that they had with them for a cargo. You never saw such sails. The tide came up and floated the ship, and they threw out anchors at bow and stern, and sat there in the sunlight, making sails and patching them and talking of the days when they were young. All this while Ivan the Ninny went walking off into the island.

Now in the middle of that island was a high mountain. A high mountain it was, and so white that when he came near it Ivan the Ninny began thinking of sheepskin coats, although it was midsummer and the sun was hot in the sky. The trees were green round about, but there was nothing growing on the mountain at all. It was just a great white mountain piled up into the sky in the middle of a

green island. Ivan walked a little way up the white slopes of the mountain, and then, because he felt thirsty, he thought he would let a little snow melt in his mouth. He took some in his fingers and stuffed it in. Quickly enough it came out again, I can tell you, for the mountain was not made of snow but of good Russian salt. And if you want to try what a mouthful of salt is like, you may.

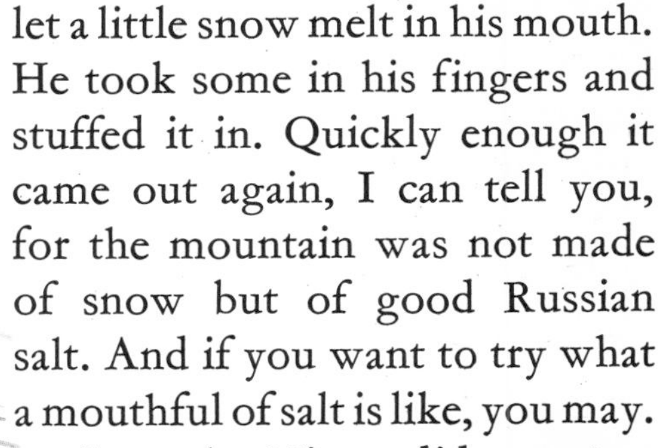

Ivan the Ninny did not stop to think twice. The salt was so clean and shone so brightly in the sunlight. He just turned round and ran back to the shore, and called out to his ancient old sailormen and told them to empty everything they had on board over into the sea. Over it all went, rags and tags and rotten timbers, till the little ship was as empty as a soup bowl after supper. And then those ancient old men were set to work carrying salt from the mountain and taking it on board the little ship, and stowing it away below deck till there was not room for another grain. Ivan the Ninny would have liked to take the whole mountain, but there was not room in the little ship. And for that the ancient old sailormen thanked God, because their backs ached and their old legs were weak, and they said they would have died if they had had to carry any more.

Then they hoisted up the new sails they had patched together out of the rags and scraps of shawls and old brocades, and they sailed away once more over the blue sea. And the wind stood fair, and they sailed before it, and the ancient old sailors rested their backs, and told old tales, and took turn and turn about at the rudder.

And after many days' sailing they came to a town with towers and churches and painted roofs, and set on the side of a hill that sloped down into the sea. At the foot of the hill was a quiet harbor, and they sailed in there and moored their ship and hauled down their patchwork sails.

Ivan the Ninny went ashore, and took with him a little bag of clean white salt to show what kind of goods he had for sale, and he asked his way to the palace of the Tzar of that town. He came to the palace, and went in and bowed to the ground before the Tzar.

"Who are you?" says the Tzar.

"I, great lord, am a Russian merchant, and here in a bag is some of my merchandise, and I beg your leave to trade with your subjects in this town."

"Let me see what is in the bag," says the Tzar.

Ivan the Ninny took a handful from the bag and showed it to the Tzar.

"What is it?" says the Tzar.

"Good Russian salt," says Ivan the Ninny.

Now in that country they had never heard of salt, and the Tzar looked at the salt, and he looked at Ivan and he laughed.

"Why, this," says he, "is nothing but white dust, and that we can pick up for nothing. The men of my town have no need to trade with you. You must be a ninny."

Ivan grew very red, for he knew what his father used to call him. He was ashamed to say anything. So he bowed to the ground, and went away out of the palace.

But when he was outside he thought to himself, "I wonder what sort of salt they use in these parts if they do not know good Russian salt when they see it! I will go to the kitchen."

So he went round to the back door of the palace, and put his head into the kitchen, and said, "I am very tired. May I sit down here and rest a little while?"

"Come in," says one of the cooks. "But you must sit just there, and not put even your little finger in the way of us; for we are the Tzar's cooks, and we are in the middle of making ready his dinner." And the cook put a stool in a corner out of the way, and Ivan slipped in round the door, and sat down in the corner and looked about him. There were seven cooks at least, boiling and baking, and stewing and toasting, and roasting and frying. And as for scullions, they were as thick as cockroaches, dozens of them, running to and fro, tumbling over each other, and helping the cooks.

Ivan the Ninny sat on his stool, with his legs tucked under him and the bag of salt on his knees. He watched the cooks and scullions, but he did not see them put anything in the dishes which he thought could take the place of salt. No; the meat was without salt, the kasha was without salt, and there was no salt in the potatoes. Ivan nearly turned sick at the thought of the tastelessness of all that food.

There came the moment when all the cooks and scullions ran out of the kitchen to fetch the silver platters on which to lay the dishes. Ivan slipped down from his stool, and running from stove to stove, from saucepan to frying pan, he dropped a pinch of salt, just what was wanted, no more no less, in every one of the dishes. Then he ran back to the stool in the corner, and sat there, and watched the dishes being put on the silver platters and carried off in gold-embroidered napkins to be the dinner of the Tzar.

The Tzar sat at the table and took his first spoonful of soup.

"The soup is very good today," said he, and he finished the soup to the last drop.

"I've never known the soup so good," says the Tzarina, and she finished hers.

"This is the best soup I ever tasted," says the Princess, and down went hers. And she, you know, was the prettiest princess who ever had dinner in this world.

It was the same with the kasha (mush) and the same with the meat. The Tzar and the Tzarina and the Princess wondered why they had never had so good a dinner in all their lives before.

"Call the cooks," said the Tzar. And they called the cooks, and the cooks all came in, and bowed to the ground, and stood in a row before the Tzar.

"What did you put in the dishes today that you never put before?" said the Tzar.

"We put nothing unusual, your greatness," said the cooks, and bowed to the ground again.

"Then why do the dishes taste better?"

"We do not know, your greatness," said the cooks.

"Call the scullions," said the Tzar. And the scullions were called, and they too bowed to the ground, and stood in a row before the Tzar.

"What was done in the kitchen today that has not been done there before?" said the Tzar.

"Nothing, your greatness," said all the scullions except one.

And that one scullion bowed again, and kept on bowing, and then he said, "Please, your greatness, please, great lord, there is usually none in the kitchen but ourselves. But today there was a young Russian merchant, who sat on a stool in the corner and said he was tired."

"Call the merchant," says the Tzar.

So they brought in Ivan the Ninny, and he bowed before the Tzar, and stood there with his little bag of salt in his hand.

"Did you do anything to my dinner?" said the Tzar.

"I did, your greatness," said Ivan.

"What did you do?"

"I put a pinch of Russian salt in every dish."

"That white dust?" said the Tzar.

"Nothing but that."

"Have you got any more of it?"

"I have a little ship in the harbor laden with nothing else," said Ivan.

"It is the most wonderful dust in the world," said the Tzar, "and I will buy every grain of it you have. What do you want for it?"

Ivan the Ninny scratched his head and thought. He thought that if the Tzar liked it as much as all that, it must be worth a fair price, so he said, "We will put the salt into bags, and for every bag of salt you must give me three bags of the same weight —one of gold, one of silver, and one of precious stones. Cheaper than that, your greatness, I could not possibly sell."

"Agreed," says the Tzar. "And a cheap price, too, for a dust so full of magic that it makes dull dishes tasty, and tasty dishes so good that there is no looking away from them."

So all the day long, and far into the night, the ancient old sailormen bent their backs under sacks of salt, and bent them again under sacks of gold and silver and precious stones. When all the salt had been put in the Tzar's treasury—yes, with twenty soldiers guarding it with great swords shining in the moonlight —and when the little ship was loaded with riches, so that even the deck was piled high with precious stones, the ancient old men lay down among the jewels and slept till morning. Then Ivan the Ninny went to bid good-by to the Tzar.

"And whither shall you sail now?" asked the Tzar.

"I shall sail away to Russia in my little ship," says Ivan.

And the Princess, who was very beautiful, said, "A little Russian ship?"

"Yes," says Ivan.

"I have never seen a Russian ship," says the Princess, and she begged her father to let her go to the harbor with her nurses and maids, to see the little Russian ship before Ivan set sail.

She came with Ivan to the harbor, and the ancient old sailormen took them on board.

She ran all over the ship, looking now at this and now at that, and Ivan told her the names of everything—deck, mast, and rudder.

"May I see the sails?" she asked. And the ancient old men hoisted the ragged sails, and the wind filled the sails and tugged.

"Why doesn't the ship move when the sails are up?" asked the Princess.

"The anchor holds her," said Ivan.

"Please let me see the anchor," says the Princess.

"Haul up the anchor, my children, and show it to the Princess," says Ivan to the ancient old sailormen.

The old men hauled up the anchor, and showed it to the Princess; and she said it was a very good little anchor. But, of course, as soon as the anchor was up the ship began to move. One of the ancient old men bent over the tiller, and, with a fair wind behind her, the little ship slipped out of the harbor and away to the blue sea. When the Princess looked round, thinking it was time to go home, the little ship was far from land. Away in the distance she could only see the gold towers of her father's palace, glittering like pin points in the sunlight. Her nurses and maids wrung their hands and made an outcry, and the Princess sat down on a heap of jewels, and put a handkerchief to her eyes, and cried and cried and cried.

Ivan the Ninny took her hands and comforted her, and told her of the wonders of the sea that he would show her, and the wonders of the land. And she looked up at him while he talked, and his eyes were kind and hers were sweet. The end of it was that they were both very well content, and agreed to have a marriage feast as soon as the little ship should bring them to the home of Ivan's father. Merry was that voyage. All day long Ivan and the Princess sat on deck and said sweet things to each other, and at twilight they sang songs, and drank tea, and told stories. As for the nurses and maids, the Princess told them to be glad; and so they danced and clapped their hands, and ran about the ship, and teased the ancient old sailormen.

That is the story about salt, and how it made a rich man of Ivan the Ninny, and, besides, gave him the prettiest wife in the world, and she a Tzar's daughter.

From *Old Peter's Russian Tales*

Rapunzel

By Jakob and Wilhelm Grimm

THERE were once a man and a woman who had long in vain wished for a child. At length the woman hoped that God was about to grant her desire. These people had a little window at the back of their house from which a splendid garden could be seen, which was full of the most beautiful flowers and herbs. But it was surrounded by a high wall, and no one dared to go into it because it belonged to a witch with great power.

One day the woman was standing by this window and looking down into the garden, when she saw a bed which was planted with the most beautiful rampion (a flower), and it looked so fresh and green that she longed for it. Her desire increased every day, and as she knew that she could not get any of it, she quite pined away, and began to look pale and miserable.

Her husband was alarmed, and asked: "What ails you?"

"Ah," she replied, "if I can't eat some of the rampion, which is in the garden behind the house, I shall die."

The man, who loved her, thought: "Sooner than let your wife die, bring her some of the rampion yourself, let it cost what it will." At twilight, he clambered down over the wall into the garden, hastily clutched a handful of rampion, and took it to his wife. She at once made herself a salad and ate it greedily. It tasted so good to her that the next day she longed for it three times as much as before.

If he was to have any rest, her husband must once more descend into the garden. In the gloom of evening, therefore, he let himself down again; but when he had clambered down the wall he was terribly afraid, for he saw the witch standing before him.

"How can you dare," said she, with angry look, "descend into my garden and steal my rampion like a thief? You shall suffer for it!"

"Ah," answered he, "let mercy replace justice. I only made

up my mind to do it out of necessity. My wife saw your rampion from the window, and felt such a longing for it that she would have died if she had not got some to eat."

Then the witch allowed her anger to be softened, and said to him: "If the case be as you say, I will allow you to take away with you as much rampion as you would like to, only I make one condition. You must give to me the child which your wife will bring into the world. It shall be well treated, and I will care for it like a mother." The man in his terror consented to everything, and when the woman had her child, the witch appeared at once, gave the baby the name of Rapunzel (which means *rampion*), and took it away with her.

Rapunzel grew into the most beautiful child under the sun. When she was twelve years old, the witch shut her into a tower which lay in a forest and had neither stairs nor door. Quite at the top was a little window. When the witch wanted to go in, she placed herself below and cried:

> Rapunzel, Rapunzel,
> Let down your hair to me.

Rapunzel had magnificent long hair, fine as spun gold. When

she heard the voice of the witch she unfastened her braided tresses, and wound them round one of the hooks of the window above. Then the hair fell twenty ells down, and the witch climbed up.

After a year or two, it came to pass that the King's son rode through the forest and passed by the tower. Then he heard a song which was so charming that he stood still and listened. This was Rapunzel, who in her solitude passed her time in letting her sweet voice resound. The King's son wanted to climb up to her, and looked for the door of the tower, but none was to be found. He rode home, but the singing had so deeply touched his heart, that every day he went out into the forest and listened to it. Once when he was thus standing behind a tree, he saw that a witch came there, and he heard her cry:

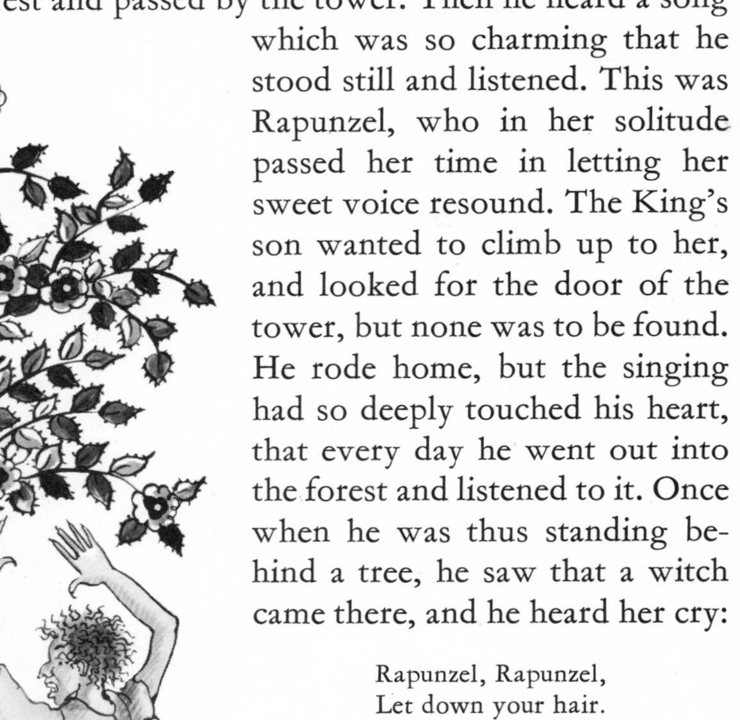

Rapunzel, Rapunzel,
Let down your hair.

Rapunzel let down her hair, and the witch climbed up.

"If that is the ladder by which one mounts, I, too, will try my fortune," said he. The next day when it began to grow dark, he went to the tower and cried:

Rapunzel, Rapunzel,
Let down your hair.

Immediately the hair fell down and the King's son climbed up.

At first Rapunzel was terribly frightened. But the King's son began to talk to her quite like a friend, and told her that his heart had been so stirred that it had let him have no rest, and he had been forced to see her. Then Rapunzel lost her fear. When he asked her if she would take him for her husband, and she saw that he was young and handsome, she thought, "He will love me more than old Dame Gothel does"; and she said yes, and laid her hand in his.

She said, "I will willingly go away with you, but I do not know how to get down. Bring with you a skein of silk every time that you come, and I will weave a ladder with it, and when that is ready I will descend, and you will take me on your horse." They agreed that until that time he should come to her every evening.

The witch remarked nothing of this, until once Rapunzel said to her: "Tell me, Dame Gothel, how it happens that you are so much heavier for me to draw up than the young King's son."

"Ah! you wicked child," cried the witch. "What do I hear you say! I thought I had separated you from all the world, and yet you have deceived me!" In her anger she clutched Rapunzel's beautiful tresses, wrapped them twice around her left hand, seized a pair of scissors with the right, and snip, snap, they were cut off, and the lovely braids lay on the ground. She took poor Rapunzel into a desert where she had to live in great grief and misery.

On the same day that she cast out Rapunzel, however, the witch fastened the braids of hair, which she had cut off, to the hook of the window, and when the King's son came and cried:

Rapunzel, Rapunzel,
Let down your hair.

she let the hair down. The King's son ascended, but instead of finding his dearest Rapunzel, he found the witch.

"Aha!" she cried, mockingly, "you would fetch your dearest, but the beautiful bird sits no longer singing in the nest. The cat has

got it, and will scratch out your eyes as well. Rapunzel is lost to you; you will never see her again."

The King's son was beside himself with pain, and in his despair he leaped down from the tower. He escaped with his life, but the thorns into which he fell pierced his eyes. Then he wandered quite blind about the forest.

Thus he roamed about in misery for some years,

and at length came to the desert where Rapunzel lived in wretchedness. He heard a voice, and it seemed so familiar to him that he went towards it. When he approached, Rapunzel knew him and fell on his neck and wept. Two of her tears wetted his eyes and they grew clear again and he could see. He led her to his kingdom and they lived for a long time afterwards, happy and contented.

From *Grimm's Fairy Tales*

Master of All Masters

Retold by JOSEPH JACOBS

A GIRL once went to the fair to hire herself for servant. At last a funny-looking old gentleman engaged her, and took her home to his house. When she got there, he told her that he had something to teach her, for in his house he had his own names for things.

He said to her: "What will you call me?"

"Master or mister, or whatever you please, sir," says she.

He said: "You must call me 'master of all masters.' And what would you call this?" pointing to his bed.

"Bed or couch, or whatever you please, sir."

"No, that's my 'barnacle.' And what do you call these?" said he, pointing to his pantaloons.

"Breeches or trousers, or whatever you please, sir."

"You must call them 'squibs and crackers.' And what would you call her?" pointing to the cat.

"Cat or kit, or whatever you please, sir."

"You must call her 'white-faced simminy.' And this now," showing the fire, "what would you call this?"

"Fire or flame, or whatever you please, sir."

"You must call it 'hot cockalorum,' and what this?" he went on, pointing to the water.

"Water or wet, or whatever you please, sir."

"No, 'pondalorum' is its name. And what do you call all this?" asked he, as he pointed to the house.

"House or cottage, or whatever you please, sir."

"You must call it 'high topper mountain.' "

That very night the servant woke her master up in a fright and said: "Master of all masters, get out of your barnacle and put on your squibs and crackers. For white-faced simminy has got a spark of hot cockalorum on its tail, and unless you get some pondalorum, high topper mountain will be all on hot cockalorum."

. . . . .That's all . . . .

Gone Is Gone

Retold by WANDA GÁG

THIS IS an old, old story which my grandmother told me when I was a little girl. When she was a little girl her grandfather had told it to her, and when he was a little peasant boy in Bohemia, his mother had told it to him. And where she heard it, I don't know, but you can see it is an old old story, and here it is, the way my grandmother used to tell it.

It is called *Gone Is Gone*

and it is the story of a man who wanted to do housework.

This man, his name was Fritzl—his wife, her name was Liesi. They had a little baby, Kinndli by name, and Spitz who was a dog.

They had one cow, two goats, three pigs, and of geese they had a dozen. That's what they had.

They lived on a patch of land, and that's where they worked.

Fritzl had to plow the ground, sow the seeds and hoe the weeds. He had to cut the hay and rake it too, and stack it up in bunches in the sun. The man worked hard, you see, from day to day.

Liesi had the house to clean, the soup to cook, the butter to churn, the barnyard and the baby to care for. She, too, worked hard each day as you can plainly see.

They both worked hard, but Fritzl always thought that he worked harder. Evenings when he came home from the field, he sat down, mopped his face with his big red handkerchief, and said: "Hu! How hot it was in the sun today, and how hard I did work. Little do you know, Liesi, what a man's work is like, little do you know! *Your* work now, 'tis nothing at all."

" 'Tis none too easy," said Liesi.

"None too easy!" cried Fritzl. "All you do is to putter and potter around the house a bit—surely there's nothing hard about such things."

"Nay, if you think so," said Liesi, "we'll take it turn and turn about tomorrow. I will do your work, you can do mine. I will go out in the fields and cut the hay, you can stay here at home and putter and potter around. You wish to try it—yes?"

Fritzl thought he would like that well enough—to lie on the grass and keep an eye on his Kinndli-girl, to sit in the cool shade and churn, to fry a bit of sausage and cook a little soup. Ho! that would be easy! Yes, yes, he'd try it.

Well, Liesi lost no time the next morning. There she was at peep of day, striding out across the fields with a jug of water in her hand and the scythe over her shoulder.

And Fritzl, where was he? He was in the kitchen, frying a string of juicy sausages for his breakfast. There he sat, holding the pan over the fire, and as the sausage was sizzling and frizzling in the pan, Fritzl was lost in pleasant thoughts.

"A mug of cider now," that's what he was thinking. "A mug of apple cider with my sausage—that would be just the thing."

No sooner thought than done.

Fritzl set the pan on the edge of the fireplace, and went down into the cellar where there was a big barrel full of cider. He pulled the bung from the barrel and watched the cider spurt into his mug, sparkling and foaming so that it was a joy to see.

But Hulla! What was that noise up in the kitchen—such a scuffle and clatter! Could it be that Spitz-dog after the sausages? Yes, that's what it was, and when Fritzl reached the top of the stairs, there he was, that dog, dashing out of the kitchen door with the string of juicy sausages flying after him.

Fritzl made for him, crying, "Hulla! Hulla! Hey, hi, ho, hulla!" But the dog wouldn't stop. Fritzl ran, Spitz ran too. Fritzl ran fast, Spitz ran faster, and the end of it was that the dog got away and our Fritzl had to give up the chase.

"Na, na! What's gone is gone," said Fritzl, shrugging his shoulders. And so he turned back, puffing and panting, and mopping his face with his big red handkerchief.

But the cider, now! Had he put the bung back in the barrel? No, that he hadn't, for here he was still holding the bung in his fist.

With big fast steps Fritzl hurried home, but it was too late, for look! the cider had filled the mug and had run all over the cellar besides.

Fritzl looked at the cellar full of cider. Then he scratched his head and said, "Na, na! What's gone is gone."

Well, now it was high time to churn the butter. Fritzl filled the churn with good rich cream, took it under a tree and began to churn with all his might. His little Kinndli was out there too, playing Moo-cow among the daisies. The sky was blue, the sun right gay and golden, and the flowers, they were like angels' eyes blinking in the grass.

"This is pleasant now," thought Fritzl, as he churned away. "At last I can rest my weary legs. But wait! What about the cow? I've forgotten all about her and she hasn't had a drop of water all morning, poor thing."

With big fast steps Fritzl ran to the barn, carrying a bucket of cool fresh water for the cow. And high time it was, I can tell you, for the poor creature's tongue was hanging out of her mouth with the long thirst that was in her. She was hungry too, as a man could well see by the looks of her, so Fritzl took her from the barn and started off with her to the green grassy meadow.

But wait! There was that Kinndli to think of—she would surely get into trouble if he went out to the meadow. No, better not take the cow to the meadow at all. Better keep her near by on the roof. The roof? Yes, the roof! Fritzl's house was not covered with shingles or tin or tile—it was covered with moss and sod, and a fine crop of grass and flowers grew there.

To take the cow up on the roof was not so hard as you might think, either. Fritzl's house was built into the side of a hill. Up the little hill, over a little shed, and from there to the green grassy roof. That was all there was to do and it was soon done.

The cow liked it right well up there on the roof and was soon munching away with a will, so Fritzl hurried back to his churning.

But Hulla! Hui! What did he see there under the tree? Kinndli was climbing up on the churn—the churn was tipping! spilling! falling! and now, there on the grass lay Kinndli, all covered with half-churned cream and butter.

"So that's the end of our butter," said Fritzl, and blinked and blinked his blue eyes. Then he shrugged his shoulders and said, "Na, na! What's gone is gone."

He picked up his dripping Kinndli and set her in the sun to dry. But the sun, now! It had climbed high up into the heavens. Noontime it was, no dinner made, and Liesi would soon be home for a bite to eat.

With big fast steps Fritzl hurried off to the garden. He gathered potatoes and onions, carrots and cabbages, beets and beans, turnips, parsley and celery.

"A little of everything, that will make a good soup," said Fritzl as he went back to the house, his arms so full of vegetables that he could not even close the garden gate behind him.

He sat on a bench in the kitchen and began cutting and paring away. How the man did work, and how the peelings and parings did fly!

But now there was a great noise above him. Fritzl jumped to his feet.

"That cow," he said, "she's sliding around right much up there on the roof. She might slip off and break her neck."

Up on the roof went Fritzl once more, this time with loops of heavy rope. Now listen carefully, and I will tell you what he did with it. He took one end of

the rope and tied it around the cow's middle. The other end of the rope he dropped down the chimney and this he pulled through the fireplace in the kitchen below.

And then? And then he took the end of the rope which was hanging out of the fireplace and tied it around his own middle with a good tight knot. That's what he did.

"Oh yo! Oh ho!" he chuckled.

"That will keep the cow from falling off the roof." And he began to whistle as he went on with his work.

He heaped some sticks on the fireplace and set a big kettle of water over it.

"Na, na!" he said. "Things are going as they should at last, and we'll soon have a good big soup! Now I'll put the vegetables in the kettle—" And that he did.

"And now I'll put in the bacon—" And that he did too.

"And now I'll light the fire—"

But that he never did, for just then, with a bump and a thump, the cow slipped over the edge of the roof after all; and Fritzl—well, he was whisked up into the chimney and there he dangled, poor man, and couldn't get up and couldn't get down.

Before long, there came Liesi home from the fields with the water jug in her hand and the scythe over her shoulder.

But Hulla! Hui! What was that hanging over the edge of the roof? The cow? Yes, the cow, and half-choked she was, too, with her eyes bulging and her tongue hanging out.

Liesi lost no time. She took her scythe—and ritsch! rotsch!—the rope was cut, and there was the cow wobbling on her four legs, but alive and well, heaven be praised!

Now Liesi saw the garden with its gate wide open. There were the pigs and the goats and all the geese too. They were full to bursting, but the garden, alas! was empty.

Liesi walked on, and now what did she see? The churn upturned, and Kinndli there in the sun, stiff and sticky with dried cream and butter.

Liesi hurried on. There was Spitz-dog on the grass. He was full of sausages and looked none too well.

Liesi looked at the cellar. There was the cider all over the floor and halfway up the stairs besides.

Liesi looked in the kitchen. The floor! It was piled high with peelings and parings, and littered with dishes and pans.

At last Liesi saw the fireplace. Hu! Hulla! Hui! What was that in the soup-kettle? Two arms were waving, two legs were kicking, and a gurgle, bubbly and weak-like, was coming up out of the water.

"Na, na! What can this mean?" cried Liesi. She did not know (but we do—yes?) that when she saved the cow outside, something happened to Fritzl inside. Yes, yes, as soon as the cow's rope was cut, Fritzl, poor man, he dropped down the chimney and crash! splash! fell right into the kettle of soup in the fireplace.

Liesi lost no time. She pulled at the two arms and tugged at the two legs—and there, dripping and spluttering, with a cabbage-leaf in his hair, celery in his pocket, and a sprig of parsley over one ear, was her Fritzl.

"Na, na, my man!" said Liesi. "Is that the way you keep house —yes?"

"Oh Liesi, Liesi!" sputtered Fritzl. "You're right—that work of yours, 'tis none too easy."

" 'Tis a little hard at first," said Liesi, "but tomorrow, maybe, you'll do better."

"Nay, nay!" cried Fritzl. "What's gone is gone, and so is my housework from this day on. Please, please, my Liesi—let me go back to my work in the fields, and never more will I say that my work is harder than yours."

"Well then," said Liesi, "if that's how it is, we surely can live in peace and happiness for ever and ever." And that they did.

Snow-White and Rose-Red

By Jakob and Wilhelm Grimm

THERE WAS once a poor widow who lived in a lonely cottage. In front of the cottage was a garden wherein stood two rose trees, one of which bore white and the other red roses. She had two children who were like the two rose trees, and one was called Snow-White, and the other Rose-Red. They were as good and happy, as busy and cheerful, as ever two children in the world were, only Snow-White was more quiet and gentle than Rose-Red. Rose-Red liked better to run about in the meadows and fields, seeking flowers and catching butterflies; but Snow-White sat at home with her mother and helped her with her housework or read to her when there was nothing to do.

The two children were so fond of each other that they always held each other by the hand when they went out together. When Snow-White said, "We will not leave each other," Rose-Red answered, "Never so long as we live," and their mother would add, "What one has she must share with the other."

They often ran about the forest alone and gathered red berries, and no beasts did them any harm, but came close to them trustfully. The little hare would eat a cabbage leaf out of their hands, the roe grazed by their side, the stag leapt merrily by them, and the birds sat still upon the boughs and sang whatever they knew.

No mishap overtook them. If they had stayed too late in the forest, and night came on, they laid themselves down near one another upon the moss and slept until morning came, and their mother knew this and had no distress on their account.

Once when they had spent the night in the wood and the dawn had roused them, they saw a beautiful child in a shining white dress sitting near their bed. He got up and looked quite kindly at them, but said nothing and went away into the forest. And, when they looked round, they found that they had been sleeping quite close to a precipice, and would certainly have fallen into it in the darkness if they had gone only a few paces farther. And their mother told them that it must have been the angel who watches over good children.

SNOW-WHITE AND ROSE-RED

Snow-White and Rose-Red kept their mother's little cottage so neat that it was a pleasure to look inside it. In the summer Rose-Red took care of the house, and every morning laid a wreath of flowers by her mother's bed before she awoke, in which was a rose from each tree. In the winter Snow-White lit the fire and hung the kettle on the crane. The kettle was of copper and shone like gold, so brightly was it polished. In the evening, when the snowflakes fell, the mother said, "Go, Snow-White, and bolt the door." Then they sat round the hearth, and the mother took her spectacles and read aloud out of a large book, and the two girls listened as they sat and spun. And close by them lay a lamb upon the floor, and behind them upon a perch sat a white dove with its head hidden beneath its wings.

One evening, as they were thus sitting comfortably together, someone knocked at the door as if he wished to be let in. The mother said, "Quick, Rose-Red, open the door. It must be a traveler who is seeking shelter." Rose-Red went and pushed back the bolt, thinking that it was a poor man, but it was not; it was a bear that stretched his broad, black head within the door.

Rose-Red screamed and sprang back, the lamb bleated, the dove fluttered, and Snow-White hid herself behind her mother's bed. But the bear began to speak and said, "Do not be afraid. I will do you no harm! I am half frozen, and only want to warm myself a little beside you."

"Poor bear," said the mother, "lie down by the fire. Only take care that you do not burn your coat." Then she cried, "Snow-White, Rose-Red, come out. The bear will do you no harm; he means well." So they both came out, and by-and-by the lamb and dove came nearer, and were not afraid of him. The bear said, "Here, children, knock the snow out of my coat a little." So they brought the broom and swept the bear's hide clean; and he stretched himself by the fire and growled contentedly and comfortably. It was not long before they grew quite at home and played tricks with their clumsy guest. They tugged at his hair with their hands, put their feet upon his back, and rolled him about; or they took a hazel switch and beat him, and when he growled they laughed. But the bear took it all in good part; only when they were too rough he called out,

> Leave me alive, children,
> Snow-White, Rosy-Red,
> Will you beat your lover dead?

When it was bedtime, and the others went to bed, the mother said to the bear, "You can lie there by the hearth, and then you will be safe from the cold and the bad weather." As soon as day dawned the two children let him out, and he trotted across the snow into the forest.

Henceforth the bear came every evening at the same time, laid himself down by the hearth, and let the children amuse themselves with him as much as they liked. They got so used to him that the doors were never fastened until their black friend had arrived.

When spring had come and all outside was green, the bear said one morning to Snow-White, "Now I must go away and cannot come back for the whole summer."

"Where are you going, then, dear bear?" asked Snow-White.

"I must go into the forest and guard my treasures from the wicked dwarfs. In the winter, when the earth is frozen hard, they are obliged to stay below and cannot work their way through. But now, when the sun has thawed and warmed the earth, they break through it, and come out to pry and steal. What once gets into their hands and in their caves does not easily see daylight again."

Snow-White was quite sorry for his going away. As she unbolted the door for him, and the bear was hurrying out, he caught against the bolt and a piece of his hairy coat was torn off. It seemed to Snow-White as if she had seen gold shining through it, but she was not sure about it. The bear ran away quickly and was soon out of sight behind the trees.

A short time afterwards the mother sent her children into the forest to get firewood. There they found a big tree which lay felled on the ground, and close by the trunk something was jumping backwards and forwards in the grass, but they could not make out what it was. When they came nearer they saw a dwarf with an old withered face and a snow-white beard a yard long. The end of the beard was caught in a crevice of the tree, and the little fellow was jumping backwards and forwards like a dog tied to a rope, and did not know what to do.

He glared at the girls with his fiery red eyes and cried, "Why do you stand there? Can you not come here and help me?"

"What are you about there, little man?" asked Rose-Red.

"You stupid, prying goose!" answered the dwarf. "I was going to split the tree to get a little wood for cooking. I had just driven the wedge safely in, and everything was going as I wished; but the wretched wood was too smooth and suddenly sprang asunder. The tree closed so quickly that I could not pull out my beautiful white beard. So now I cannot get away, and the silly, sleek, milk-faced things laugh! Ugh! How odious you are!"

The children tried very hard, but they could not pull the beard out; it was caught too fast. "I will run and fetch someone," said Rose-Red.

"You senseless goose!"

snarled the dwarf. "Why should you fetch someone? You are already two too many for me. Can you not think of something better?"

"Don't be impatient," said Snow-White. "I will help you." And she pulled her scissors out of her pocket, and cut off the end of the beard.

As soon as the dwarf felt himself free, he laid hold of a bag which lay among the roots of the tree, and which was full of gold, and lifted it up, grumbling to himself, "Uncouth people, to cut off a piece of my fine beard. Bad luck to you!" Then he swung the bag upon his back and went off without even looking at the children.

Some time after that Snow-White and Rose-Red went to catch a dish of fish. As they came near the brook they saw something like a large grasshopper jumping towards the water, as if it were going to leap in. They ran to it and found it was the dwarf. "Where are you going?" said Rose-Red. "You surely don't want to go into the water?"

"I am not such a fool!" cried the dwarf. "Don't you see that the accursed fish wants to pull me in?" The little man had been sitting there fishing, and unluckily the wind had twisted his beard with the fishline. Just then a big fish bit, and the feeble creature had not strength to pull it out. The fish kept the upper hand and pulled the dwarf towards him. He held on to all the reeds and rushes, but it was of little good. He was forced to follow the movements of the fish, and was in danger of being dragged into the water.

The girls came just in time. They held him fast and tried to free his beard from the line, but all in vain. Beard and line were entangled fast together. Nothing was left but to bring out the scissors and cut the beard, whereby a small part of it was lost. When the dwarf saw that he screamed out, "Is that civil, you toadstool, to disfigure one's face? Was it not enough to clip off the end of my beard? Now you have cut off the best part of it. I cannot let myself be seen by my people. I wish you had been made to run the soles off your shoes!" Then he took out a sack of pearls which lay in the rushes, and without saying a word more he dragged it away and disappeared behind a stone.

It happened that soon afterwards the mother sent the two children to the town to buy needles and thread and laces and ribbons. The road led them across a heath upon which huge pieces of rock lay strewn here and there. Now they noticed a large bird hovering in the air, flying slowly round and round above them. It sank lower and lower and at last settled near a rock not far off. Directly afterwards they heard a loud, piteous cry. They ran up and saw with horror that the eagle had seized their old acquaintance, the dwarf, and was going to carry him off.

The children, full of pity, at once took tight hold of the little man and pulled against the eagle so long that at last he let his booty go. As soon as the dwarf had recovered from his first fright, he cried with his shrill voice, "Could you not have done it more carefully! You dragged at my brown coat so that it is all torn and full of holes, you helpless clumsy creatures!" Then he took up a sack full of precious stones, and slipped away again under the rock into his hole. The girls, who were used to his thanklessness, went on their way and did their business in the town.

As they crossed the heath again on their way home they surprised the dwarf, who had emptied out his bag of precious stones in a clean spot, and had not thought that anyone would come there so late. The evening sun shone upon the brilliant stones; they glittered and sparkled with all colors so beautifully that the children stood still and looked at them.

"Why do you stand gaping there?" cried the dwarf.

He was going on with his bad words when a loud growling was heard, and a black bear came trotting towards them out of the forest. The dwarf sprang up in a fright, but he could not get to his cave, for the bear was already close. Then in the dread of his heart he cried, "Dear Mr. Bear, spare me. I will give you all my treasures; look, the beautiful jewels lying there! Grant me my life.

What do you want with such a slender little fellow as I? You would not feel me between your teeth. Come, take these two wicked girls; they are tender morsels for you, fat as young quails. For mercy's sake, eat them!" The bear gave the wicked creature a single blow with his paw, and he did not move again.

The girls had run away, but the bear called to them, "Snow-White and Rose-Red, do not be afraid. Wait, I will come with you." Then they knew his voice and waited; and when he came up to them suddenly his bearskin fell off, and he stood there a handsome man, clothed all in gold. "I am a king's son," he said, "and I was bewitched by that wicked dwarf, who had stolen my treasures. I have had to run about the forest as a savage bear until I was freed by his death."

Snow-White was married to him, and Rose-Red to his brother, and they divided between them the great treasure which the dwarf had gathered in his cave.

From *Household Tales*, translated by
Margaret Hunt

Sleeping Beauty

By Jakob and Wilhelm Grimm

A LONG time ago there lived a King and Queen, who said every day, "If only we had a child!" But for a long time they had none.

One day, as the Queen was bathing, a frog crept out of the water on to the land and said to her, "Your wish shall be fulfilled. Before a year has passed you shall bring a daughter into the world."

The frog's words came true. The Queen had a little girl who was so beautiful that the King could not contain himself for joy. He prepared a great feast and invited all his relations and friends and neighbors. He invited the fairies, too, in order that they might be kind and good to the child. There were thirteen of them in the kingdom, but as the King had only twelve golden plates for them to eat from, one of the fairies had to be left out.

The feast was held with all splendor, and when it came to an end, each of the fairies presented the child with a magic gift. One fairy gave her virtue, another beauty, a third riches, and so on, with everything in the world that she could wish for.

When eleven of the fairies had said their say, the thirteenth suddenly appeared. She wanted to show her spite for not having been invited. Without greeting anyone, or even glancing at anyone, she called out in a loud voice,

"When she is fifteen years old, the Princess shall prick herself with a spindle and shall fall down dead."

Then without another word she turned and left the hall.

Everyone was terror-stricken, but the twelfth fairy, whose wish was still not spoken, stepped forward. She could not take away the curse, but could only soften it, so she said,

"Your daughter shall not die, but shall fall into a deep sleep lasting a hundred years."

The King was so anxious to guard his dear child from this misfortune that he sent out a command that all the spindles in the whole kingdom should be burned.

All the promises of the fairies came true. The Princess grew up so beautiful, modest, kind, and clever that everybody who saw her could not but love her.

Now it happened that on the very day when she was fifteen years old the King and Queen were away from home, and the Princess was left quite alone in the castle. She wandered about over the whole place, looking at rooms and halls as she pleased, and at last she came to an old tower. She went up a narrow, winding staircase and reached a little door. A rusty key was sticking in the lock, and when she turned it the door flew open.

In a little room sat an old woman with a spindle, busily spinning her flax. This old woman was so deaf that she had never heard the King's command that all spindles should be destroyed.

"Good day, Granny," said the Princess, "what are you doing?"

"I am spinning," said the old woman, and nodded her head.

"What is the thing that whirls round so merrily?" asked the Princess, and she took the spindle and tried to spin, too.

But she had scarcely touched the spindle when it pricked her finger. At that moment she fell upon the bed which was standing near, and lay still in a deep sleep.

The King and Queen, who had just come home and had stepped into the hall, fell asleep, too, and all their courtiers with them. The horses fell asleep in the stable, the dogs in the yard, the doves on the roof, the flies on the wall. Yes, even the fire on the hearth grew still and went to sleep, and the meat that was roasting stopped crackling. The kitchen maid, who sat with a fowl before her, ready to pluck its feathers, fell asleep. The cook, too, who was pulling the kitchen boy's hair because he had made a mistake, let him go and both fell asleep. The wind dropped, and on the trees in front of the castle not a leaf stirred.

Round the castle a hedge of brier roses began to grow up. Every year it grew higher, till at last nothing could be seen of the castle.

There was a legend in the land about the lovely Sleeping Beauty, as the King's daughter was called, and from time to time Princes came and tried to force a way through the hedge into the castle. But they found it impossible, for the thorns, as though they had hands, held them fast, and the Princes remained caught in them without being able to free themselves, and so died.

After many, many years a Prince came again to the country and heard an old man tell of the castle which stood behind the brier hedge, in which a most beautiful maiden called Sleeping Beauty had been asleep for the last hundred years, and with her slept the King and Queen, and all their courtiers. He knew, also, from his grandfather, that many Princes had already come and sought to pierce through the brier hedge, and had been caught in it and died.

Then the young Prince said, "I am not afraid. I must go and see this Sleeping Beauty."

The good old man did all in his power to persuade him not to go, but the Prince would not listen to his words.

Now the hundred years were just ended. When the Prince approached the brier hedge it was covered with beautiful large blossoms. The shrubs made way for him of their own accord and let him pass unharmed, and then closed up again into a hedge.

In the courtyard he saw the horses and dogs lying asleep. On the roof sat the doves with their heads under their wings. When he went into the house the flies were asleep on the walls. Near the throne lay the King and Queen. In the kitchen the cook still had his hand raised as though to strike the kitchen boy, and the maid sat with the black fowl before her ready to pluck its feathers.

He went on farther. All was so still that he could hear his own breathing. At last he reached the tower, and opened the door into the little room where the Princess was asleep. There she lay, looking so beautiful that he could not take his eyes off her. He bent down and gave her a kiss. As he touched her, Sleeping Beauty opened her eyes and smiled at him.

Then they went down together. The King and the Queen and all the courtiers woke up, and looked at each other with astonished eyes. The horses in the stable stood up and shook themselves. The hounds leaped about and wagged their tails. The doves on the roof lifted their heads from under their wings, looked around, and flew into the fields. The flies on the walls began to crawl again. The fire in the kitchen roused itself and blazed up and cooked the food. The meat began to crackle, and the cook woke up and boxed the kitchen boy's ears so that he screamed aloud, while the maid finished plucking the fowl.

Then the Prince and Sleeping Beauty were married with all splendor, and they lived happily all their lives.

Cinderella

Retold by KATHARINE GIBSON

ONCE upon a time, four sisters lived in a small house. The first sister dressed in silk and the second sister in satin, and the third had lace on all her petticoats. But the youngest was in rags, and because she spent so much time cleaning and scrubbing the ashes from the hearth, she was called Cinderella.

The first sister was tall and thin, and had a long, sharp nose and a sharp chin. The second sister was round and fat, and had squinting eyes and a flat nose. The third sister was bent and twisted, and had a bitter tongue.

But Cinderella, for all her rags, was beautiful. Her golden hair floated light as the wind over her shoulders. Under her black lashes her eyes were blue. Her cheeks, though often streaked with tears and ashes, were smooth and pink.

One day the King's heralds appeared in the village square. They blew on their trumpets and spoke with loud brassy voices:

"Hear ye, hear ye! At full noon, a fortnight and one day from this day, His Royal Highness the Prince will have reached his twenty-first birthday. His Majesty the King does now declare a grand Ball to be held in his honor. Hear ye, hear ye!"

What a rustle and bustle! The milliner was soon all out of feathers. Not a spool of ribbon was left in the village. Only cotton and calico remained on the shelves in the shops. Every inch of silk, satin, broadcloth, and gold braid was sold the first day. Dressmakers and tailors stitched and sewed until their needles pushed through their thimbles. Makers of fine boots and slippers never slept at all. Hairdressers curled and frizzed or snapped and clicked with their long bright scissors day and night.

"I shall wear a purple gown," said the first sister.

"I shall wear a green," said the second.

"As for me," said the third, "mine will be mustard yellow."

"Sisters," sighed Cinderella, "you have so many dresses. If only I could borrow an old one and go to the Ball!"

"You go to the Ball? Who ever heard of such a thing?"

"A cinder wench, indeed!"

"Besides, you're much too young."

On the night of the Ball, the three sisters swept off to the King's palace, with skirts rustling, fans waving, feathers fluttering.

Cinderella sat by the cold hearth in rags, her toes in the ashes. Tears trickled down her cheeks and made a pool beside the broom.

Suddenly she heard a swish like the sound of wings in the air. A dark shadow went swiftly past. Cinderella looked up with wide, startled eyes.

On the hearth beside her stood a little old woman all in black, astride a broomstick. She wore a wide cape and a high-crowned black hat, and on her shoulder sat an owl-eyed black cat. As though dismounting from a horse, she hopped off her broomstick.

"Why are you sitting there in the ashes crying?" asked the little old woman sharply.

"Who—who are you?" asked Cinderella.

"You wait and see," the old woman said. Underneath her wide-brimmed hat her eyes shone bright as blue fire.

"Why, I say, are you crying?"

"My three sisters—everyone has gone to the Prince's Ball. Only I am left behind!" At this, Cinderella hid her face in her hands and began to sob.

"I suppose you think you'll get there by crouching in the dust and doing nothing about it."

"No," said Cinderella. "No, I don't expect to go at all."

"Are there," asked the little old woman, "any rats in the trap?"

"Any what?" Cinderella was astonished at the question.

"Don't stand there looking at me. I said, have you any rats in the trap?"

"Why, yes, six—three in the trap in the barn, and three in the trap in the loft—and two gray field mice in the trap in the pantry."

"Get the traps and put them just outside the garden gate."

Cinderella wondered a great deal, but she ran quickly to do as she was told. The little old woman followed her into the garden.

"And now," she said, "get me the largest pumpkin in the field." Wondering still more, Cinderella hastened to do the little old woman's bidding. She brought a large round pumpkin, golden as the harvest moon.

"Put it beside the traps."

Suddenly, before Cinderella's eyes, the pumpkin changed into a golden coach. The six fat, black rats changed into six fat, black, prancing horses. The field mice changed, one into a footman, one into a coachman. Both wore gray velvet suits and gray velvet hats.

Before her wide and shining eyes, Cinderella saw the little old woman reach out for a handful of moonbeams. With a swift, weaving motion, she made of them a gown that gleamed and shone.

In a trice Cinderella's rags were gone; light as a butterfly's wing, the gown slipped over her shoulders. On her feet were tiny glass slippers.

"Cinderella," said the little old woman, shaking her broomstick, "when the clock strikes twelve, you must leave the Ball. If you do not, the horses will be rats and the footmen will be mice; the coach will be a pumpkin, and you, my fine lady, will be a cinder wench, all in rags. See that you do not forget."

"I will not forget. But who are you?" asked Cinderella.

"I am your Fairy Godmother. Make sure that you remember."

"I will remember, Fairy Godmother."

Before she could thank the little old woman, Cinderella saw a shadow pass over the treetops; her Fairy Godmother was gone.

When the coach arrived at the palace and Cinderella stepped out, the servingmen were so astonished that buttons popped off all their tight waistcoats. Their eyes were round with wonder as Cinderella, as if gowned in starlight, floated past them.

When the Prince saw her, he left a Duchess in purple and

ermine standing in the center of the ballroom floor. Nor did he dance with any other, once he had taken Cinderella by the hand.

So lighthearted was Cinderella, so charming the Prince, so bewitching the music, that when the town clock struck the first note of twelve Cinderella did not hear it. But at the second, she seemed to see among the dancers a little old woman all in black with a high-crowned black hat.

Cinderella gave a cry of fear and fled in an instant. What was the Prince's astonishment to find himself quite alone in the great ballroom! He searched in vain for the beautiful Princess with whom he had danced all evening.

Cinderella fled through the palace gardens and was safely in her coach as the clock struck the final note of twelve.

The next morning the three sisters could talk of nothing but the strange Princess.

"The Prince would dance with no one else," said the eldest.

"Why he danced with her, no one knows. She was certainly no handsomer than many another, and she wore no plumes at all." The second sister shook her head.

"Did the Prince dance with no other?" asked Cinderella.

"You mind the fire!" snapped the first sister.

But the third sister said with a sigh, "At the stroke of twelve the music stopped, the ballroom grew dark. The Prince cared for nothing after the strange Princess left."

When she heard this, Cinderella smiled happily at the hearth broom.

But the Prince was so sad at the loss of the Princess that the King declared a second Ball should be given. On the evening chosen by the King, again the three sisters went proudly off to the castle in their laces and satins. Again Cinderella rode in her fairy coach.

The Prince welcomed Cinderella with such rapture that she could think of nothing but his smiles. Nor would he move from her side, though a Queen and two Empresses had traveled many miles in the hope that he would notice them.

Nine, rang the town clock—*ten, eleven.* On the first stroke of twelve Cinderella was still dancing with the Prince, and on the third and fourth. Then a tiny whisper reached her ear; it was fainter than the chirp of a cricket.

"When the clock strikes twelve, you must leave the Ball. If you do not, the horses will be rats, and the footmen, mice; the coach will be a pumpkin. . . ."

Cinderella, pale with fright, did not wait to hear the rest. On the fifth stroke of twelve, the Prince found himself alone. Cinderella rushed through shining halls, through corridors ablaze with crystal chandeliers. Swiftly the Prince followed; more swiftly ran Cinderella.

From the head of the palace steps the Prince saw a cinder

wench all in rags go weeping into the darkness. Six black rats went scampering off to hunt for the King's cheese; two gray field mice whisked briskly after. A large pumpkin rolled down the palace hill toward the village. It was golden as the towers of the King's castle.

Look as he might, the Prince could not find his Princess. Sadly he mounted the steps, when suddenly his eye caught a sparkle before him—a flickering gleam like that of a lost jewel. Kneeling, he picked up a tiny glass slipper which he could easily hold in the palm of his hand. He wrapped it in his long velvet sleeve, for with this and this alone could he find Cinderella.

So sad was the Prince in the days that followed that he would neither eat nor sleep. The King sent messengers far and near to find one whose foot was so small that she could wear the glass slipper. For the Prince would wed none other.

The morning after the second Ball, Cinderella, all in rags, went about her hard tasks. But always she dreamed of the Prince. Her three older sisters were crosser than ever.

"Who ever heard of such a thing?"

"The Prince did not dance with us."

"He danced only with that same strange Princess. She's the daughter of the Lord of all the Indies—or so they say."

"Her dress was woven of diamond threads."

"Daughter of the Lord of all the Indies?" asked Cinderella.

"You scrub that floor! What are Princes to you?" The older sister shook her head until her curl papers nearly fell off.

For days and days the King's heralds searched the country. To great cities they went, to small towns and villages. Everywhere the women gathered in eager groups, each one more anxious than the other to become the Prince's wife.

At last the heralds came to the little square where Cinderella lived with her three sisters. The heralds' suits were of scarlet and

gold. Their long brass trumpets shone in the sun. Streamers of many colors blew in the breeze from their standards. The women, young and old, fair and dark, soft-voiced or shrill, clustered about the heralds like a flock of quarreling sparrows. But none could get on the glass slipper. At last the heralds stood before Cinderella's door.

"Hear ye, hear ye! She who can wear the glass slipper shall wed the Prince. Hear ye!"

The first sister tried, but only her big toe would go in. The second sister pushed in two toes. The third squeezed in three.

"Let me try," said Cinderella.

"You—a princess!" mocked her sisters.

"Likely the Prince would wed rags and tatters!"

"Queen of the dusty hearth!"

As the sisters laughed and tossed their heads, the King's chief

herald knelt before Cinderella. The glass slipper fitted! It shone upon her foot like a star among the ashes!

"You are the Princess!" cried the herald. "Come with us, Your Highness!"

Cinderella went with the heralds to the palace. All the folk crowded after her, the men wondering, the women weeping with envy.

When the Prince looked upon Cinderella he did not see her rags or the ashes on her cheek. He saw only her golden hair, her wide blue eyes. He saw one foot bare, one foot twinkling in the glass slipper.

Commanded by the King, the heralds blew once more on their trumpets: "The Princess has been found! Tomorrow the royal pair will be married. Hear ye, hear ye!"

The wedding feast lasted ten days and ten nights. Cinderella's sisters danced only with stable grooms. As for Cinderella and the Prince, they lived happily ever after.

Hansel and Gretel

Translated by WANDA GÁG

IN A LITTLE hut near the edge of a deep, deep forest lived a poor woodchopper with his wife and his two children, Hansel and Gretel.

Times were hard. Work was scarce and the price of food was high. Many people were starving, and our poor woodchopper and his little brood fared as badly as all the rest.

One evening after they had gone to bed, the man said to his wife, "I don't know what will become of us. All the potatoes are gone, every head of cabbage is eaten, and there is only enough rye meal left for a few loaves of bread."

"You are right," said his wife, who was not the children's real mother, "and there is nothing for us to do but take Hansel and Gretel into the woods and let them shift for themselves."

She was a hard-hearted woman and did not much care what became of the children. But the father loved them dearly and said, "Wife, what are you saying? I would never have the heart to do such a thing!"

"Oh well then," snapped the stepmother, "if you won't listen to reason, we'll all have to starve." And she nagged and scolded until the poor man, not knowing what else to say, consented to do it. "May heaven keep them from harm," he sighed.

Hunger had kept the children awake that night, and, lying in their trundle beds on the other side of the room, they had heard every word their parents had said. Gretel began to cry softly but her brother Hansel whispered, "Don't worry, little sister; I'll take care of you."

He waited until the father and mother were sleeping soundly. Then he put on his little jacket, unbarred the back door and slipped out. The moon was shining brightly, and the white pebbles which lay in front of the house glistened like silver coins. Hansel bent down and gathered as many of the shiny pebbles as his pockets would hold. Then he tiptoed back to bed and told Gretel he had thought of a very good plan for the morrow.

At break of day the mother came to wake the children. "Get up, you lazy things," she said, "we're off to the forest to gather wood. Here is a piece of bread for each of you. Don't eat it until noon; it's all you'll get today."

Gretel carried both pieces of bread in her apron because, of course, Hansel's pockets were so full of pebbles. They were soon on their way to the forest: the mother first with a jug of water, the father next with an ax over his shoulder, Gretel with the bread, and Hansel bringing up the rear, his pockets bulging with

pebbles. But Hansel walked very slowly. Often he would stand still and look back at the house.

"Come, come, Hansel!" said the father. "Why do you lag behind?"

"I'm looking at my little white kitten, papa. She's sitting on the roof and wants to say good-by."

"Fool!" said the mother. "That's not your kitten. That's only the morning sun shining on the chimney."

But Hansel lingered on and dropped the pebbles behind him, one at a time, all along the way.

It was a long walk, and Hansel and Gretel became very tired. At last the mother called a halt and said, "Sit down, children, and rest yourselves while we go off to gather some wood. If you feel sleepy you can take a little nap."

Hansel and Gretel sat down and munched their bread. They thought their father and mother

were near by, because they seemed to hear the sound of an ax. But what they heard was not an ax at all, only a dry branch which was bumping against a dead tree in the wind.

By and by the two little children became so drowsy they lay down on the moss and dropped off to sleep. When they awoke it was night and they were all alone.

"Oh, Hansel, it's so dark! Now we'll never find our way home," said Gretel, and began to cry.

But Hansel said, "Don't cry, little sister. Just wait until the moon is out; I'll find the way home."

The moon did come out, full and round and bright, and it shone on the white pebbles which Hansel had strewn along the way. With the glistening pebbles to guide them, they found their way back easily enough.

Dawn was stealing over the mountains when they reached their home, and with happy faces they burst in at the door. When their mother saw them standing before her, she was taken aback.

But then she said, "Why, you naughty children! Where have you been so long? I began to think you didn't want to come back home."

She wasn't much pleased but the father welcomed them joyfully. He had lain awake all night worrying over them.

* * *

Luckily, things now took a turn for the better, and for several weeks the woodchopper was able to earn enough money to keep his family from starving. But it did not last, and one evening the children, still awake in their trundle beds, heard the mother say to the father: "I suppose you know there's only one loaf of bread left in the house, and after that's eaten, there's an end to the song. We must try once more to get rid of the children, and this time we'll take them still deeper into the woods, so our sly Hansel can't find his way back."

As before, the father tried to talk her out of it, but the hard-hearted stepmother wouldn't listen to him. He who says A must also say B, and because the father had given in the first time, he had to give in this time as well.

Hansel saw that he would have to get up and gather pebbles again, and as soon as his parents were asleep, he crept out of bed. But alas! the door was locked now and he had to go back to bed and think of a different plan.

The next day everything happened as it had the first time. Hansel and Gretel were each given a crust of bread and then they all went forth into the forest. Hansel brought up the rear as before, and kept straggling behind the rest.

"Come, come, Hansel!" said the father. "Why do you lag behind?"

"I see my pet dove, papa. It is sitting on the roof and wants to say good-by to me."

"Fool!" said the mother. "That's not your dove. That's only the morning sun shining on the chimney."

But Hansel kept on loitering because he was again busy making a trail to guide them back home. And what do you think he did this time? He had broken his bread crust into tiny pieces and now he was carefully scattering the crumbs, one by one, behind him on the path.

They had to walk even farther than before, and again the parents went to gather wood, leaving Hansel and Gretel behind. At noon Gretel shared her bread with Hansel, and then they both fell asleep.

When they awoke, it was dark and they were all alone. This time Gretel did not cry because she knew Hansel had scattered crumbs to show them the way back. When the moon rose, Hansel took her hand and said, "Come, little sister, now it's time to go home."

But alas! when they looked for the crumbs they found none. Little twittering birds which fly about in the woods and glades, had eaten them all, all up.

* * *

The two unhappy children walked all that night and the next day too, but the more they looked for the way, the more they lost it. They found nothing to eat but a few sour berries; and at last, weak and hungry, they sank down on a cushion of moss and fell asleep.

It was now the third morning since they had left their home. They started to walk again, but they only got deeper and deeper into the wood.

They felt small and strange in the large, silent forest. The trees were so tall and the shade was so dense. Flowers could not grow in that dim, gloomy place—not even ferns. Only pale waxy mushrooms glowed faintly among the shadows, and weird lichens clung to the tree trunks. Suddenly, into the vast green silence fell a ripple of sound so sweet, so gay, so silvery, that the children looked up in breathless wonder. A little white bird sat there in a tree; and when its beautiful song was ended, it spread its wings and fluttered away with anxious little chirps as though it wished to say, "Follow me! Follow me!"

Hansel and Gretel followed gladly enough, and all at once they found themselves in a fair flowery clearing, at the edge of which stood a tiny cottage.

The children stood hand in hand and gazed at it in wonder. "It's the loveliest house I ever saw," gasped Gretel, "and it looks good enough to eat."

They hurried on, and as they reached the little house, Hansel touched it and cried, "Gretel! It *is* good enough to eat."

And, if you can believe it, that's just what it was. Its walls were made of gingerbread, its roof was made of cake. It was trimmed with cookies and candy, and its windowpanes were of pure transparent sugar. Nothing could

have suited the children better and they began eating right away, they were so hungry! Hansel plucked a cookie from the roof and took a big bite out of it. Gretel munched big slabs of sugarpane which she had broken from the window.

Suddenly a honeyed voice came floating from the house. It said:

Nibble, nibble, nottage,
Who's nibbling at my cottage?

To which the children said mischievously:

It's only a breeze,
Blowing down from the trees.

At this, the door burst open, and out slithered a bent old woman, waggling her head and leaning on a knotted stick. Hansel stopped munching his cookie and Gretel stopped crunching her sugarpane. They were frightened—and no wonder! The Old One was far from beautiful. Her sharp nose bent down to meet her bristly chin. Her face, all folds and wrinkles, looked like an old shriveled pear; and she had only three teeth, two above and one below, all very long and yellow.

When the Old One saw that the children were turning to run away, she said in sugary tones, "Ei, ei! my little darlings, what has brought you here? Come right in and stay with me. I'll take good care of you."

She led them inside, and there in the middle of the room was a table neatly spread with toothsome dainties: milk, pancakes and honey, nuts, apples and pears.

While the children were eating their fill, the Old One made up two little beds which stood at one end of the room. She fluffed up the feather bed and puffed up the pillows, she turned back the lily-white linen, and then she said: "There, my little rabbits—a downy nest for each of you. Tumble in and slumber sweetly."

As soon as Hansel and Gretel were sound asleep, the Old One walked over and looked at them.

"Mm! Mm! Mm!" she said. "They're mine for certain!"

Now why should she do that? Well, I must tell you the real truth about the Old One. She wasn't as good and friendly as she pretended to be. She was a bad, bad witch who had built that sweet and sugary house on purpose to attract little children. Witches have ruby-red eyes and can hardly see at all, but oh! how they can smell with those long sharp noses of theirs! What they can smell is human beings; and that morning, as Hansel and Gretel were wandering around in the forest, the Old One knew it well enough. Sniff! sniff! sniff! went her nose—she had been sniffing and waiting for them all day.

The next morning while the two little innocents were still sleeping peacefully, the Old One looked greedily at their round arms and rosy cheeks. "Mm! Mm! Mm!" she mumbled. "Juicy morsels!"

She yanked Hansel out of bed, dragged him into the back yard, and locked him up in the goose-coop. Hansel screamed and cried but it did him no good.

Then the Old One went into the house, gave Gretel a rough shake and cried,"Up with you, lazy bones. Make haste and cook some food for your brother. He's out in the goose-coop and if we feed him well, ei! ei! what a tasty boy he'll make!"

When Gretel heard this she burst into tears, but the Old One gave her a cuff on the ears and said, "Stop howling, you fool. Pick up your legs and do as I tell you."

Each day Gretel had to cook big pots full of fattening food for Hansel, and each morning the Old One hobbled out to the goose-coop and cried, "Hansel, let me see your finger so I can tell how fat you're getting."

But Hansel never showed her his finger. He always poked out a dry old bone, and the Old One, because of her red eyes, never knew

the difference. She thought it really was his finger, and wondered why it was that he did not, did not get fat.

When four weeks had passed and Hansel seemed to stay thin, the Old One became impatient and said to Gretel, "Hey there, girl! Heat up a big kettle of water. I'm tired of waiting and, be he fat or lean, I'm going to have Hansel for my supper tonight."

Gretel cried and pleaded with her. But the Old One said, "All that howling won't do you a bit or a whit of good. You might as well spare your breath."

She built a roaring fire in the stove and said to Gretel, "First we'll do some baking. I've mixed and kneaded the dough, and the loaves are all ready for the oven." Then she opened the oven door and added in a sweet voice, "Do you think it's hot enough for the bread, Gretel dear? Just stick your head in the oven and see, there's a good girl!"

Gretel was about to obey, when a bird (the same white bird which had led them out of the forest) began to sing a song. It seemed to Gretel he was singing:

> Beware, beware,
> Don't look in there.

So Gretel didn't look into the oven. Instead she said to the Old One, "Well, I really don't know how to go about it. Couldn't you first show me how?"

"Stupid!" cried the Old One. "It's easy enough. Just stick your head way in and give a good look around. See? Like this!"

As the Old One poked her horrid old head into the oven, Gretel gave her a push and a shove, closed the oven door, bolted it swiftly and ran away. The Old One called and cried, and frizzled and fried, but no one heard. That was the end of her, and who cares?

Gretel was already in the back yard. "Hansel!" she cried. "We are free!" She opened the door of the goose-coop and out popped Hansel. The children threw their arms about each other.

* * *

But now there came a soft whirr in the air. The children stopped dancing and looked up. The good white bird and many others—all the twittering birds from the fields and glades—were settling on the cake-roof of the gingerbread house.

On the roof was a nest full of pearls and sparkling gems. Each little forest-bird took out a pearl or a gem and carried it down to the children. Hansel held out his hands, and Gretel held up her apron to catch all these treasures, while the little white bird sat on the roof and sang:

Thank you for the crumbs of bread,
Here are gems for you instead.

Now Hansel and Gretel understood that these were the very same birds who had eaten up their crumbs in the forest, and that this was how they wished to show their thanks.

As the birds fluttered away, Hansel said, "And now, little sister, we must make haste and get out of this witchy wood. As for me, I got very homesick sitting in that goose-coop week after week."

"And I," said Gretel. "Yes, I've been homesick too. But, Hansel, how can we ever find our way back?"

Ho, what luck! There was the little white bird fluttering ahead of them once more. It led them away and soon they were in a green meadow. In front of them lay a big, big pond. How to get over it! As Hansel and Gretel stood on the shore wondering what to do, a large swan came floating by, and the children said:

Float, swan, float!
Be our little boat.

The swan dipped its graceful head, raised it and dipped it again —that meant yes. When the swan had taken the children, one by one, to the other shore, they thanked it prettily and patted its long curved neck. Near the water's edge ran a neat little path. Hansel and Gretel followed it, and now the trees and the fields began to

look familiar. Soon they saw their father's house gleaming through the trees and they ran home as fast as they could. As the door burst open and his two little ones ran in with shouts and laughter, his eyes filled with tears of joy. He hugged them and all he could say was: "My treasures, my little treasures!"

"Oh, as to treasures, papa," said Hansel, putting his hands into his pockets, "we'll show you some! See, now we will never have to starve again." At this, Gretel poured a shower of jewels from her apron, while Hansel added handful after handful from his pockets.

And the hard-hearted stepmother, where was she? Well, I'll tell you. When Hansel and Gretel seemed to be gone for good, the woman saw that her husband could think of nothing but his lost children. This made her so angry that she packed up her things in a large red handkerchief and ran away.

From *Tales from Grimm*

Aladdin and the Wonderful Lamp

ALADDIN was the son of a poor tailor in one of the rich cities of China. His father died while Aladdin was yet very young, and his mother had to spin cotton day and night in order to support herself and him.

One day when he was about fifteen years old, he was playing in the streets with some of his companions. A stranger who was passing by stopped to look at him. This stranger was an African magician who was in need of the help of some young person. He knew at once that Aladdin was the boy who would be able to help him.

The magician first asked Aladdin's name of some persons standing near by. Then he went up to him and said, "My lad, are you not the son of Mustapha, the tailor?"

"Yes, sir," answered the boy, "but my father has been dead a long time."

At these words the magician threw his arms about Aladdin's neck, and with tears in his eyes, he said, "I am your uncle. Your father was my own brother. I knew you at first sight; you are so like him."

Then he gave Aladdin two pieces of gold, saying, "Go, my son, to your mother, and tell her that I will sup with her tonight."

Pleased with the money, Aladdin ran to his mother.

"Mother," said he, "have I an uncle?"

"No, child," replied his mother. "Your father had no brother, nor have I."

"I am just now come," said Aladdin, "from a man who says he is my father's brother. He gave me money and said that he would sup with you tonight."

The good woman was much surprised, but went out and bought food, and spent the day in preparing a supper. Just as the meal was ready, the magician knocked at the door, and came in loaded with all sorts of fruits and sweetmeats. He saluted Aladdin's mother, and with tears in his eyes, asked to be shown the place where his brother used to sit. As soon as they sat down to supper, he began to tell of his travels.

"My good sister," said he, "do not be surprised that you have never seen me before. I have been forty years away from this country, and during that time I have traveled in many lands. I am indeed sad to learn of my brother's death, but it is a comfort to find that he has so fine a son."

Then turning to Aladdin, he asked, "What business do you follow? Are you of any trade?"

Aladdin hung his head, and had nothing to say.

His mother replied, "Aladdin has never learned a trade. He does nothing but idle away his time in the streets."

"That is not well, Nephew," said the magician. "You must think of some way of earning a living. I will be glad to help you. If you like, I will take a shop for you and furnish it with fine linens."

Aladdin was full of joy at the idea. He told the magician that no business would please him better.

"Well, then," said the magician, "I will take you with me to-morrow, and clothe you as handsomely as any merchant in the city. Then we will open a shop."

He came again the next day, as he had promised, and took Aladdin to a merchant who sold all sorts of clothes. Aladdin chose those he liked best and put them on. The magician then took the boy to visit the finest shops in the city, and in the evening he gave him a feast.

When Aladdin's mother saw him return so well dressed, and heard him tell all that had happened, she was much pleased.

"Kind brother," said she to the magician, "I do not know how to thank you for all your goodness."

"Aladdin," he replied, "is a good boy, and well deserves all that I can do for him. I shall be very proud of him some day. To-morrow I want to take him to see the gardens outside the town, and then the next day we will open the shop."

Aladdin rose very early the next morning, and ran to meet his uncle when he saw him coming. The magician led the boy out at one of the gates of the city to some beautiful gardens. They walked on and on, talking as they went, until they had gone far into the country.

When they grew tired, they sat down by a fountain of clear water, and the magician took from his girdle a box filled with cakes and fruits.

When they had eaten, they walked farther into the country, until they came to a narrow valley, with mountains on all sides. This was the place that the magician had hoped to reach. He had brought Aladdin here for a secret purpose.

"We will go no farther now," he said to the boy. "I will show you here some strange things that no one besides yourself will ever see. While I strike a light, gather up all the loose dry sticks you can see, to kindle a fire with."

Aladdin had soon gathered a great pile. The magician set fire to the wood, and when the flames arose, he threw in some incense. He then spoke two magic words, which Aladdin did not understand.

At once the earth opened at their feet. They could see a great stone with a brass ring fixed in it. Aladdin was so frightened that he would have run away, but the magician held him.

"If you will obey me," he said, "you will not be sorry. Under this stone there is hidden a treasure which will make you richer than all the kings in the world. But you must do exactly what I say."

Aladdin's fear was now gone, and he said, "Well, Uncle, what is to be done? I am ready to obey."

"Take hold of the ring," said the magician, "and lift up that stone."

Aladdin did as the magician told him, raised the stone and laid it on one side. When the stone was pulled up, there appeared a staircase three or four feet deep, leading to a door.

"Go down those steps," said the magician, "and open that door. It will lead you into a palace, divided into three great halls. In each of these you will see four vases full of gold and silver, but do not meddle with them. You must pass through the three halls without stopping. Above all, be very careful not to go near the outer walls, or even to touch them with your robe, for if you do so, you will die instantly.

"At the end of the third hall, you will find a door, which opens into a garden full of beautiful trees loaded with fruit. Walk across the garden to a wall, where you will see a niche before you, and in that niche a lighted lamp. Take the lamp down and put it out. Then throw away the wick and oil, and bring me the lamp."

After these words, the magician drew a ring from his finger, and put it on one of Aladdin's, saying, "This will protect you

against all evil, so long as you obey me. Go now, my son; do as I have told you, and we shall both be rich all our lives."

Aladdin went down the steps, and opened the door. He found the three halls, just as the magician had said. He went through them carefully, and crossed the garden without stopping. He took the lamp from the niche, threw away the wick and the oil, and put the lamp in his girdle.

As he started back, he stopped in the garden to look at the fruit. The trees were loaded with fruits of different colors. Some were white, and others sparkled like crystals. Some were red and some green; some were blue, and others were violet. The white fruits were pearls; the sparkling ones were diamonds. The red ones were rubies; the green, emeralds; the blue, turquoises; and the purple, amethysts.

Aladdin did not know their value, and thought they were only glass. But the beautiful colors pleased him, and he gathered some of each kind. He filled both his pockets and his leather bag, too.

Loaded with the treasure, he hurried through the halls, and soon arrived at the mouth of the cavern. He saw the magician waiting for him, and called out,

"Give me your hand, Uncle, and help me out."

"First, give me the lamp," said the magician, "so that it may not hinder you."

"Indeed, Uncle," replied the lad, "I cannot now, but I will as soon as I am out."

The magician was determined that he would have the lamp before he would help the boy up. But Aladdin was so burdened with the fruit of the trees that he could not well get at the lamp.

The magician then flew into a rage, threw a little incense upon the fire, and spoke two magic words. At once the stone returned to its own place, and closed up the entrance of the strange cavern.

When Aladdin found himself in darkness, he called to the

magician, telling him a thousand times that he would give him the lamp, but his cries were useless. He went to the bottom of the steps, thinking to enter the garden again, but the door was now shut.

For two days Aladdin remained in darkness without eating or drinking. At last he clasped his hands in prayer, and in so doing, he rubbed the ring which the magician had put upon his finger.

At once an enormous and frightful genie rose out of the earth, saying, "What do you wish? I am the slave of the ring, and will obey you in all things."

Aladdin replied, "Take me from this place."

At once the earth opened, and he found himself outside. He went home, but fell fainting at the door. When he came to himself, he told his mother what had passed, and showed her the lamp and the fruits he had gathered. He then asked for some food.

"Alas, child," she said, "I have nothing in the house, but I have spun a little cotton, and will go and sell it."

"Keep the cotton, Mother," said Aladdin, "and sell the lamp instead."

She took the lamp and began to rub it, for it was very dusty.

Instantly a frightful genie appeared, and cried with a loud voice, "What will you have? I am the slave of the lamp, and will obey those who hold it."

Aladdin's mother was too frightened to speak, but Aladdin seized the lamp, and said boldly, "Fetch me something to eat." The genie vanished, and in a moment returned, bearing on his head a silver tray. On the tray were twelve silver dishes filled with the finest food. There were also two silver plates and two silver cups. He placed the tray upon the table and again vanished.

Aladdin and his mother sat down and ate in great delight. Never before had they tasted such delicious food. When they had eaten all that the genie had brought, they sold the silver dishes, one by one, and got more food. In this way they lived well for some time.

One day, as he was walking in the city, Aladdin heard an order of the Sultan, telling all persons to close their shops and go into their houses while the Princess, his daughter, passed on her way to the bath.

Aladdin hid himself behind a door where he might see the Princess as she passed. He had not long to wait before she came with a great crowd of her maids. As she drew near the door where Aladdin was hiding, she threw aside her veil, and he saw her face. She was so beautiful that he loved her at first sight.

When Aladdin told his mother of his love for the Princess, she laughed and said, "Alas! My son, what can you be thinking of? You must be mad to talk thus."

"I am not mad," said Aladdin, "but in my right senses. I am determined to ask the Princess in marriage from the Sultan. You must go before him today to win his favor."

"I!" cried his mother. "I go to the Sultan! You know very well

that no one can go before the Sultan without a rich gift, and where shall I find one?"

"Ah," said Aladdin, "I have a secret to tell you. Those bits of glass which I got from the trees in the cavern are jewels of great value. I have looked at the precious stones in all the shops, and none are so large and beautiful as mine. The offer of them, I am sure, will win the favor of the Sultan."

Then Aladdin brought the stones from the chest where they had been hidden, and his mother placed them in a fine china dish. The beauty of their colors amazed the mother, and she was certain that the gift could not fail to please the Sultan. She folded the dish and the jewels in a fine linen cloth, and set out to the

palace of the Sultan.

The crowd of those who had business at the court was very great. The doors were opened, and she went in with the others, and placed herself in front of the Sultan. He, however, took no notice of her. She went every day for a week, and stood in the same place.

At last he sent for her and asked what she wanted of him. Trembling, the good woman told him of Aladdin's wish. The Sultan heard her kindly, and then asked her what she had in the napkin. She unfolded the cloth, and laid before him the sparkling jewels.

What was the surprise of the Sultan when he saw those jewels! For a long time he gazed at them without speaking. Then he exclaimed, "How very rich! How very beautiful!"

The Sultan, however, had planned that his daughter should marry one of his own officers, and so he said to Aladdin's mother, "Tell your son that he shall marry my daughter, if he will send to me forty golden basins filled with jewels like these. They must be brought to me by forty black slaves, each of whom shall be led by a white slave, all richly dressed. Tell him that I await his answer."

The mother of Aladdin bowed low, and went home, thinking that all was lost. She gave Aladdin the message, adding, "He may wait long enough for his answer."

Aladdin smiled, and when his mother had gone out, he took the lamp and rubbed it. The genie instantly appeared, and Aladdin bade him bring the present that the Sultan had asked.

The genie vanished, and soon returned with forty black slaves, each carrying upon his head a golden basin filled with pearls, diamonds, rubies, and emeralds. The forty black slaves and the forty white slaves filled the house and the garden behind.

Aladdin bade them set out to the palace, two and two, and asked his mother to follow and present his gift to the Sultan.

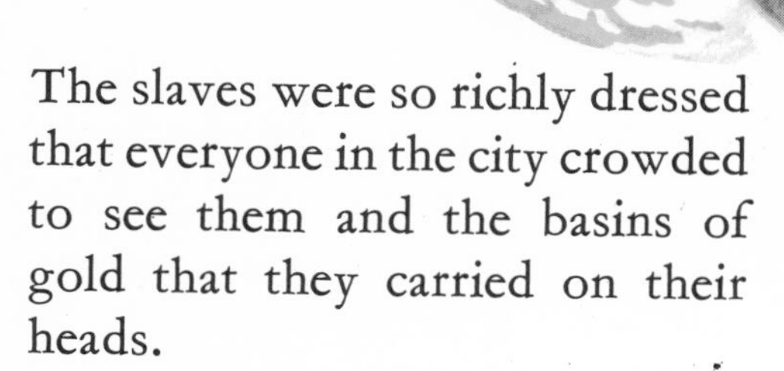

The slaves were so richly dressed that everyone in the city crowded to see them and the basins of gold that they carried on their heads.

They entered the palace and knelt before the Sultan. Each of the black slaves placed his basin upon the carpet, and then they stood in a semicircle about the throne.

The astonishment of the Sultan at the sight of these riches cannot be told. After gazing at the shining heaps of jewels, he finally roused himself and said to Aladdin's mother,

"Go, my good woman, and tell your son that I am waiting with open arms to welcome him."

The happy woman lost no time in giving the message to Aladdin, bidding him make haste. But Aladdin first called the genie.

"I want a scented bath," said

he, "a rich robe, a horse as splendid as the Sultan's, and twenty slaves to attend me; and besides, twenty thousand pieces of gold in twenty purses."

All was done at once. Aladdin in a rich robe mounted his horse, and passed through the streets. Ten slaves marched on either side of him, and each carried a purse of gold to scatter among the people.

When the Sultan saw the handsome young man, he came down from his throne to greet him, and led him into a hall, where a great feast was spread. He wished Aladdin to marry his daughter, but Aladdin said, "I must first build a palace fit for her."

As soon as he reached home, he called the genie, and said, "Build me a palace of the finest marble, set with precious stones. There must be stables and horses and grooms and slaves."

The next morning the genie appeared and carried Aladdin to the palace. It was far more beautiful than Aladdin had hoped. Indeed, the Sultan and all his household were filled with wonder.

The marriage of Aladdin and the Princess was held the same day amid great rejoicing. Aladdin had won the love of the people by his kindness, and he lived for a time in great happiness.

Far away in Africa the magician found out by his magic arts that Aladdin was very rich and much beloved, instead of being dead in the cave. Filled with rage, he set out for China.

As he passed through the city, he heard everyone talking of the wonderful palace. He knew that it had been raised by the genie of the lamp, and he determined to get the lamp at any cost.

He was told by the merchants that Aladdin had gone a-hunting, and would not return for three or four days.

The magician then bought a dozen copper lamps, and went to the palace crying, "New lamps for old!"

When he came under the window of the Princess, all the slaves laughed as they heard the cry.

"Come," said one, "let us see if the old man means what he says. There is an ugly old lamp on the shelf. We will ask him to give us a new one in its place."

Now this was the magic lamp, which Aladdin had left there when he went hunting. The Princess, not knowing its value, laughed, and bade the slave take it and make the exchange.

The magician gladly gave for it the best lamp that he had, and then hurried away to the forest. When night came, he called the genie of the lamp, and commanded that the palace, the Princess, and he himself be carried before day to the farthest corner of Africa.

The grief of the Sultan was terrible when he found that the palace and his daughter had disappeared. Soldiers were sent to find Aladdin, who was brought bound before the Sultan. He would have been beheaded, had not the people begged for his life.

"I will spare your life," said the Sultan, "for forty days. Within that time you must find my daughter, or you will lose your head."

Aladdin wandered about like a madman, asking everyone that he met what had become of his palace, but the people only laughed at him. At last he stopped at a little brook to drink some water. He made a cup of his hands, and in so doing rubbed the magic ring, which he still wore upon his finger.

The genie of the ring appeared, and asked his will.

"O mighty genie," cried Aladdin, "bring back my palace."

"That is not in my power," said the genie. "You must ask the slave of the lamp. I am only the slave of the ring."

"Then," said Aladdin, "take me where the palace is."

Instantly he found himself in a strange country, standing beside his own palace. The Princess was even then walking in her room, weeping. As she looked out of the window, she saw Aladdin, and she was filled with joy. She called to him to come to her, and she told him all that had happened.

When Aladdin heard of the exchange of the lamps, he knew

at once that the magician was the cause of all his sorrow.

"Tell me," he asked, "where is the old lamp now?"

"The tyrant carries it in his girdle," said the Princess, "and never parts with it, by day or by night."

They talked together, and laid a plan for getting back the lamp. Aladdin went into the city and bought a powder that would cause instant death. The Princess dressed herself in rich robes, and invited the magician to sup with her.

While they were at the table, she ordered a slave to bring two cups of wine which she had prepared. The magician, pleased by her kindness, gladly drank the wine she gave him, and at once fell dead.

Aladdin, who was hiding near by, seized the lamp and called the genie, bidding him to carry the palace back to China.

A few hours later, the Sultan, looking from his window, saw Aladdin's palace sparkling in the sun. He ordered a great feast to be made ready, and there was merrymaking for a whole week.

After this Aladdin and his wife lived in peace. When the Sultan died, Aladdin ascended the throne, and ruled for many years.

From *The Arabian Nights*

The Ugly Duckling

By Hans Christian Andersen

THE COUNTRY was very lovely just then—it was summer. The wheat was golden and the oats still green. The hay was stacked in the rich low meadows, where the stork marched about on his long red legs, chattering in Egyptian, the language his mother had taught him.

Round about the field and meadow lay great woods, in the midst of which were deep lakes. Yes, the country certainly was lovely. In the sunniest spot stood an old mansion surrounded by a deep moat, and great dock leaves grew from the walls of the house right down to the water's edge. Some of them were so tall that a small child could stand upright under them. In among the leaves it was as secluded as in the depths of a forest, and there a duck was sitting on her nest. Her ducklings were just about to be hatched, but she was quite tired of sitting, for it had lasted such a long time. Moreover, she had very few visitors, as the other ducks liked swimming about in the moat better than waddling

up to sit under the dock leaves and gossip with her.

At last one egg after another began to crack. "Cheep, cheep!" they said. All the chicks had come to life and were poking their heads out.

"Quack, quack!" said the duck, and then they all quacked their hardest and looked about them on all sides among the green leaves. Their mother allowed them to look as much as they liked, for green is good for the eyes.

"How big the world is, to be sure!" said all the young ones. They now had ever so much more room to move about than when they were inside their eggshells.

"Do you imagine this is the whole world?" said the mother. "It stretches a long way on the other side of the garden, right into the parson's field, though I have never been as far as that. I suppose you are all here now?" She got up and looked about. "No, I declare I have not got you all yet! The biggest egg is still there. How long is this going to take?" she said, and settled herself on the nest again.

"Well, how are you getting on?" asked an old duck who had come to pay her a visit.

"This one egg is taking such a long time!" answered the sitting duck. "The shell will not crack. But now you must look at the others. They are the finest ducklings I have ever seen. They are all exactly like their father, the rascal! Yet he never comes to see me."

"Let me look at the egg which won't crack," said the old duck. "You may be sure that it is a turkey's egg! I was cheated like that once and I had no end of trouble and worry with the creatures, for I may tell you that they are afraid of the water. I simply could not get them into it. I quacked and snapped at them, but it all did no good. Let me see the egg! Yes, it is a turkey's egg. You just leave it alone, and teach the other children to swim."

"I will sit on it a little longer. I have sat so long already that I may as well go on till the Midsummer Fair comes round."

"Please yourself," said the old duck, and away she went.

At last the big egg cracked. "Cheep, cheep!" said the young one and tumbled out. How big and ugly he was! The duck looked at him.

"That is a monstrous big duckling," she said. "None of the others looked like that. Can he be a turkey chick? Well, we shall soon find that out. Into the water he shall go, if I have to kick him in myself."

The next day was gloriously fine, and the sun shone on all the green dock leaves. The mother duck with her whole family went down to the moat.

Splash! Into the water she sprang. "Quack, quack," she said, and one duckling after another plumped in. The water dashed over their heads, but they came up again and floated beautifully. Their legs went of themselves, and they were all there. Even the big ugly gray one swam about with them.

"No, that is no turkey," she said. "See how beautifully he uses his legs and how erect he holds himself. He is my own chick, after all, and not bad looking when you come to look at him properly. Quack, quack! Now come with me and I will take you out into the world and introduce you to the duckyard. But keep close to me all the time, so that no one may tread upon you. And beware of the cat!"

Then they went into the duckyard. There was a fearful uproar going on, for two broods were fighting for the head of an eel, and in the end the cat captured it.

"That's how things go in this world," said the mother duck, and she licked her bill, because she wanted to have the eel's head herself.

"Use your legs," said she. "Mind you quack properly, and

bend your necks to the old duck over there. She is the grandest of us all. She has Spanish blood in her veins and that accounts for her size. And do you see? She has a red rag round her leg. That is a wonderfully fine thing, and the most extraordinary mark of distinction any duck can have. It shows clearly that she is not to be parted with, and that she is worthy of recognition both by beasts and men! Quack, now! Don't turn your toes in! A well-brought-up duckling keeps his legs wide apart just like father and mother. That's it. Now bend your necks and say quack!"

They did as they were bid, but the other ducks round about looked at them and said, quite loudly, "Just look there! Now we are to have that tribe, just as if there were not enough of us already. And, oh dear, how ugly that duckling is! We won't stand him." And a duck flew at him at once and bit him in the neck.

"Let him be," said the mother. "He is doing no harm."

"Very likely not," said the biter. "But he is so ungainly and queer that he must be whacked."

"Those are handsome children mother has," said the old duck with the rag round her leg. "They are all good looking except this one. He is not a good specimen. It's a pity you can't make him over again."

"That can't be done, your grace," said the mother duck. "He is not handsome, but he is a thoroughly good creature, and he swims as beautifully as any of the others. I think I might venture even to add that I think he will improve as he goes on, or perhaps in time he may grow smaller. He was too long in the egg, and so he has not come out with a very good figure." And then she patted his neck and stroked him down.

"The other ducklings are very pretty," said the old duck. "Now make yourselves quite at home, and if you find the head

of an eel you may bring it to me."

After that they felt quite at home. But the poor duckling which had been the last to come out of the shell, and who was so ugly, was bitten, pushed about, and made fun of by both the ducks and the hens. "He is too big," they all said. The poor duckling was at his wit's end, and did not know which way to turn. He was in despair because he was so ugly and the butt of the whole duckyard.

So the first day passed, and afterwards matters grew worse and worse. The poor duckling was chased and hustled by all of them. Even his brothers and sisters ill-used him. They were always saying, "If only the cat would get hold of you, you hideous object!" Even his mother said, "I wish to goodness you were miles away." The ducks bit him, the hens pecked him, and the girl who fed them kicked him aside.

Then he ran off and flew right over the hedge, where the little birds flew up into the air in a fright.

"That is because I am so ugly," thought the poor duckling, shutting his eyes, but he ran on all the same. Then he came to a great marsh where the wild ducks lived. He was so tired and miserable that he stayed there the whole night. In the morning the wild ducks flew up to inspect their new comrade.

"What sort of a creature are you?" they inquired, as the duckling turned from side to side and greeted them as well as he could. "You are frightfully ugly," said the wild ducks, "but that does not matter to us, so long as you do not marry into our family."

Poor fellow! He had not thought of marriage. All he wanted was permission to lie among the rushes and to drink a little of the marsh water.

He stayed there two whole days. Then two wild geese came, or rather two wild ganders. They were not long out of the shell and therefore rather pert.

"I say, comrade," they said, "you are so ugly that we have taken quite a fancy to you! Will you join us and be a bird of passage? There is another marsh close by, and there are some charming wild geese there. All are sweet young ladies who can say quack! You are ugly enough to make your fortune among them." Just at that moment, "bang! bang!" was heard up above, and both the wild geese fell dead among the reeds, and the water turned blood red. "Bang! bang!" went the guns, and whole flocks of wild geese flew up from the rushes and the shots peppered among them again.

There was a grand shooting party, and the sportsmen lay hidden round the marsh. Some even sat on the branches of the trees which overhung the water. The blue smoke rose like clouds among the dark trees and swept over the pool.

The retrieving dogs wandered about in the swamp—splash! splash! The rushes and reeds bent beneath their tread on all sides. It was terribly alarming to the poor duckling. He twisted his head round to get it under his wing, and just at that moment a frightful big dog appeared close beside him. His tongue hung right out of his mouth, and his eyes glared wickedly. He opened his great chasm of a mouth close to the duckling, showed his sharp teeth, and—splash!—went on without touching him.

"Oh, thank Heaven!" sighed the duckling. "I am so ugly that even the dog won't bite me!"

Then he lay quite still while the shots whistled among the bushes, and bang after bang rent the air. Late in the day the noise ceased, but even then the poor duckling did not dare to get up. He waited several hours more before he looked about, and then he hurried away from the marsh as fast as he could. He ran across fields and meadow, and there was such a wind that he had hard work to make his way.

Towards night he reached a poor little cottage. It was such a miserable hovel that it remained standing only because it could not make up its mind which way to fall. The wind whistled so fiercely round the duckling that he had to sit on his tail to resist it, and it blew harder and ever harder. Then he saw that the door had fallen off one hinge and hung so crookedly that he could creep into the house through the crack, and by this means he made his way into the room.

An old woman lived here with her cat and her hen. The cat, whom she called, "Sonnie," could arch his back, purr, and even give off sparks, though for that you had to stroke his fur the wrong way. The hen had quite tiny short legs, and so she was called "Chickie-low-legs." She laid good eggs, and the old woman was as fond of her as if she had been her own child.

In the morning the strange duckling was discovered immediately, and the cat began to purr and the hen to cluck.

"What on earth is that?" said the old woman, looking round, but her sight was not good and she thought the duckling was a fat duck which had escaped. "This is a wonderful find!" said she. "Now I shall have duck's eggs—if only it is not a drake. We must wait and see about that."

So she took the duckling on trial for three weeks, but no eggs made their appearance. The cat was master of this house and the hen its mistress. They always said, "We and the world," for they thought that they represented the half of the world, and that quite the better half.

The duckling thought there might be two opinions on the subject, but the hen would not hear of it.

"Can you lay eggs?" she asked.

"No."

"Have the goodness to hold your tongue then!"

And the cat said, "Can you arch your back, purr, or give off sparks?"

"No."

"Then you had better keep your opinions to yourself when people of sense are speaking!"

The duckling sat in the corner nursing his ill humor. Then he began to think of the fresh air and the sunshine, and an uncontrollable longing seized him to float on the water. At last he could not help telling the hen about it.

"What on earth possesses you?" she asked. "You have nothing to do. That is why you get these freaks into your head. Lay some eggs or take to purring, and you will get over it."

"But it is so delicious to float on the water," said the duckling. "It is so delicious to feel it rushing over your head when you dive to the bottom."

"That would be a fine amusement!" said the hen. "I think you have gone mad. Ask the cat about it. He is the wisest creature I know. Ask him if he is fond of floating on the water or diving under it. I say nothing about myself. Ask our mistress herself, the old woman. There is no one in the world cleverer than she is. Do you suppose she has any desire to float on the water or to duck underneath it?"

"You do not understand me," said the duckling.

"Well, if we don't understand you, who should? I suppose you don't consider yourself cleverer than the cat or the old woman, not to mention me! Don't make a fool of yourself, child, and thank your stars for all the good we have done you. Have you not lived in this warm room, and in such society that you might have learned something? But you are an idiot, and there is no pleasure in associating with you. You may believe me; I mean you well. I tell you home truths, and there is no surer way than that of knowing who are one's friends. You just set about laying some eggs, or learn to purr, or to emit sparks."

"I think I will go out into the wide world," said the duckling.

"Oh, do so by all means," said the hen.

So away went the duckling. He floated on the water and ducked underneath it, but he was looked askance at and slighted by every living creature for his ugliness. Now the autumn came on. The leaves in the woods turned yellow and brown. The wind took hold of them, and they danced about. The sky looked very cold and the clouds hung heavy with snow and hail. A raven stood on the fence and croaked, "Caw, caw!" from sheer cold. It made one shiver only to think of it. The poor duckling certainly was in a bad case!

One evening, the sun was just setting in wintry splendor when a flock of beautiful large birds appeared out of the bushes. The duckling had never seen anything so beautiful. They were dazzlingly white with long waving necks. They were swans, and uttering a peculiar cry they spread out their magnificent broad wings and flew away from the cold regions to warmer lands and open seas. They mounted so high, so very high, and the ugly little duckling became strangely uneasy. He circled round and round in the water like a wheel, craning his neck up into the air after them. Then he uttered a shriek so piercing and so strange that he was quite frightened by it himself.

Oh, he could not forget those beautiful birds, those happy birds. And as soon as they were out of sight he ducked right down to the bottom, and when he came up again he was quite beside himself. He did not know what the birds were, or whither they flew, but all the same he was more drawn towards them than he had ever been by any creatures before. He did not envy them in the least. How could it occur to him even to wish to be such a marvel of beauty? He would have been thankful if only the ducks would have tolerated him among them—the poor ugly creature.

The winter was so bitterly cold that the duckling was obliged to swim about in the water to keep it from freezing over, but

every night the hole in which he swam got smaller and smaller. Then it froze so hard that the surface ice cracked, and the duckling had to use his legs all the time so that the ice should not freeze around him. At last he was so weary that he could move no more, and he was frozen fast into the ice.

Early in the morning a peasant came along and saw him. He went out onto the ice and hammered a hole in it with his heavy wooden shoe, and carried the duckling home to his wife. There he soon revived. The children wanted to play with him, but the duckling thought they were going to ill-use him. In his fright he rushed into the milk pan, and the milk spurted out all over the room. The woman shrieked and threw up her hands. Then he flew into the butter cask, and down into the meal tub and out again. Just imagine what he looked like by this time! The woman screamed and tried to hit him with the fire tongs. The children tumbled over one another in trying to catch him, and they screamed with laughter. By good luck the door stood open, and the duckling flew out among the bushes and the newly fallen snow. And he lay there thoroughly exhausted.

But it would be too sad to mention all the privation and misery he had to go through during the hard winter. When the sun began to shine warmly again, the duckling was in the marsh, lying among the rushes. The larks were singing and the beautiful spring had come.

Then all at once he raised his wings and they flapped with much greater strength than before and bore him off vigorously. Before he knew where he was, he found himself in a large garden where the apple trees were in full blossom and the air was scented with lilacs, long branches of which overhung the shores of the lake. Oh, the spring freshness was delicious!

Just in front of him he saw three beautiful white swans advancing towards him from a thicket. With rustling feathers they swam lightly over the water. The duckling recognized the majestic birds, and he was overcome by a strange melancholy.

"I will fly to them, the royal birds, and they will hack me to pieces because I, who am so ugly, venture to approach them. But it won't matter! Better be killed by them than be snapped at by the ducks, pecked by the hens, spurned by the hen wife, or suffer so much misery in the winter."

So he flew into the water and swam towards the stately swans. They saw him and darted towards him with ruffled feathers.

"Kill me!" said the poor creature, and he bowed his head towards the water and awaited his death. But what did he see reflected in the transparent water?

He saw below him his own image, but he was no longer a clumsy dark gray bird, ugly and ungainly. He was himself a swan!

He felt quite glad of all the misery and tribulation he had gone through, for he was the better able to appreciate his good fortune now and all the beauty which greeted him. The big swans swam round and round him and stroked him with their bills.

Some little children came into the garden with corn and pieces of bread which they threw into the water, and the smallest one cried out, "There is a new one!" The other children shouted with joy, "Yes, a new one has come." And they clapped their hands and danced about, running after their father and mother. They threw the bread into the water, and one and all said, "The new one is the prettiest of them all. He is so young and handsome." And the old swans bent their heads and did homage before him.

He felt quite shy, and hid his head under his wing. He did not know what to think. He was very happy, but not at all proud, for a good heart never becomes proud. He thought of how he had been pursued and scorned, and now he heard them all say that he was the most beautiful of all beautiful birds. He raised his slender neck aloft, saying with exultation in his heart, "I never dreamt of so much happiness when I was the Ugly Duckling!"

AESOP'S
FABLES

The Town Mouse and the Country Mouse

By Aesop

NOW you must know that a Town Mouse once upon a time went on a visit to his cousin in the country. He was rough and ready, this cousin, but he loved his town friend and made him heartily welcome. Beans and bacon, cheese and bread, were all he had to offer, but he offered them freely.

The Town Mouse rather turned up his long nose at this country fare, and said, "I cannot understand, Cousin, how you can put up with such poor food as this, but of course you cannot expect anything better in the country. Come you with me and I will show you how to live. When you have been in town a week, you will wonder how you could ever have stood a country life."

No sooner said than done: the two mice set off for the town and arrived at the Town Mouse's residence late at night.

"You will want some refreshment after our long journey," said the polite Town Mouse, and took his friend into the grand dining room.

There they found the remains of a fine feast, and soon the two mice were eating up jellies and cakes and all that was nice.

Suddenly they heard growling and barking.

"What is that?" asked the Country Mouse.

"It is only the dogs of the house," answered the other.

"Only!" said the Country Mouse. "I do not like that music at my dinner."

Just at that moment the door flew open, in came two huge mastiffs, and the two mice had to scamper down and run off.

"Good-by, Cousin," said the Country Mouse.

"What! Going so soon?" said the other.

"Yes," replied the Country Mouse,

"Better beans and bacon in peace than cakes and ale in fear."

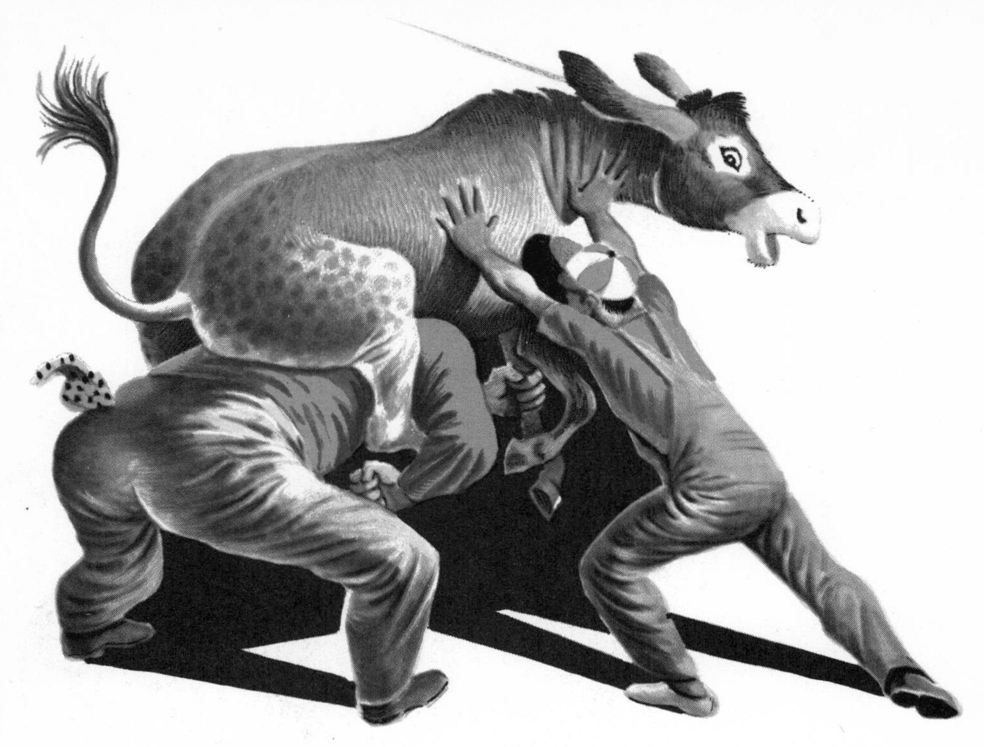

The Farmer, His Son, and the Donkey

By Aesop

A FARMER and his young Son were traveling to market with their Donkey. Down a country road they met some gossiping farm girls who giggled and jeered at them, "Have you ever seen such fools? Walking when they might be riding!"

The Farmer then bade his Son, "Jump on the back of the Donkey and ride. We don't want to appear ridiculous."

The Son did so. Presently they passed through a village where, in front of the inn, some old men were sunning themselves.

"Just look at that," they grumbled. "There is a fine example of what the younger generation is coming to. That young sprout rides, while his poor old father wears his life away walking!"

"Perhaps they are right, my son," said the Farmer. "It might look better if I ride and you walk."

He mounted the Donkey, and they had proceeded a mile along the road when they encountered some countrywomen with their children.

"The cruelty of some fathers to their children is frightful!" exclaimed the women. "That lazy oaf rides, while his poor son, barely able to keep up with him, limps behind."

"Jump up behind me, son," bade the Farmer. "I shouldn't like to be thought a cruel father!"

So, both on the back of the Donkey, they entered the market town.

"Oho!" shouted the other farmers. "What a poor, maltreated beast, carrying a double burden. I wouldn't treat an animal of mine like that. They should be arrested, those two! Why, they would be better able to carry the Donkey than he them!"

So the Farmer and his Son dismounted, and between them picked up the Donkey and carried him. As they were going over a bridge, the uncomfortable Donkey began to kick himself free with such energy that they all fell into the water.

It is futile to try to keep up appearances before everybody.

From *Aesop's Fables*, edited by Elizabeth Stones

Belling the Cat

By Aesop

LONG ago, the mice held a general council to consider what measures they could take to outwit their common enemy, the Cat. Some said this, and some said that, but at last a young mouse got up and said he had a proposal to make which he thought would meet the case.

"You will all agree," said he, "that our chief danger consists in the sly and treacherous manner in which the enemy approaches us. Now, if we could receive some signal of her approach, we could easily escape from her. I venture, therefore, to propose that a small bell be procured, and attached by a ribbon round the neck of the Cat. By this means we should always know when she was about, and could easily retire while she was in the neighborhood."

This proposal met with general applause, until an old mouse got up and said,

"That is all very well, but who is to bell the Cat?"

The mice looked at one another and nobody spoke. Then the old mouse said,

"It is easy to propose impossible remedies."

The Crow and the Pitcher

By Aesop

A CROW, half-dead with thirst, came upon a pitcher which had once been full of water; but when the Crow put his beak into the mouth of the pitcher he found that only very little water was left in it, and that he could not reach far enough down to get at it. He tried and he tried, but at last had to give up in despair.

Then a thought came to him, and he took a pebble and dropped it into the pitcher. Then he took another pebble and dropped it into the pitcher. Then he took another pebble and dropped that into the pitcher. Then he took another pebble and dropped that into the pitcher. Then he took another pebble and dropped that into the pitcher. Then he took another pebble and dropped that into the pitcher. At last, at last, he saw the water mount up near him, and after casting in a few more pebbles he was able to quench his thirst and save his life.

Little by little does the trick.

The Fox and the Stork

By Aesop

AT ONE time the Fox and the Stork were on visiting terms and seemed very good friends. So the Fox invited the Stork to dinner, and for a joke put nothing before her but some soup in a very shallow dish. This the Fox could easily lap up, but the Stork could only wet the end of her long bill in it, and left the meal as hungry as when she began.

"I am sorry," said the Fox, "the soup is not to your liking."

"Pray do not apologize," said the Stork. "I hope you will return this visit, and come and dine with me soon."

So a day was appointed when the Fox should visit the Stork, but when they were seated at table all there was for their dinner was contained in a very long-necked jar with a narrow mouth, in which the Fox could not insert his snout. So all he could manage to do was to lick the outside of the jar.

"I will not apologize for the dinner," said the Stork:

"One bad turn deserves another."

The Lion and the Mouse

By Aesop

ONCE when a Lion was asleep a little Mouse began running up and down upon him. This soon wakened the Lion, who placed his huge paw upon the little Mouse, and opened his big jaws to swallow him.

"Pardon, O King," cried the little Mouse, "let me go this time and I shall never forget it. Who knows but what I may be able to do you a good turn some of these days?"

The Lion was so tickled at the idea of the Mouse being able to help him, that he lifted up his paw and let him go.

Some time later the Lion was caught in a trap. The hunters, who desired to carry him alive to the King, tied him to a tree while they went in search of a wagon to carry him on. Just then the little Mouse happened to pass by and, seeing the sad plight in which the Lion was, went up to him and soon gnawed away the ropes that bound the King of Beasts.

"Was I not right?" said the little Mouse.

Little friends may prove great friends.

The Dog and the Bone

By Aesop

ONE DAY a Dog, carrying a bone in his mouth, was crossing a bridge. Glancing down, he caught sight of his reflection in the smooth water. But he thought it was another dog and, greedy for the other's bone, began to bark. As soon as he opened his mouth his own bone dropped into the water and was lost forever.

It is wiser to take care of your own possessions than to be greedy for those of others.

From *Aesop's Fables*, edited by Elizabeth Stones

The Maid and the Milk Can

By Aesop

A DAIRYMAID was going to market one day, a milk can balanced on her head. On the way, she began to calculate the profit she would make out of the sale of her milk.

"With this money," she meditated, "I shall be able to buy quite a number of eggs. Of course, they won't all be good ones, but at least three quarters of them will produce chickens. Some of these I shall take to market and sell, and with the money I shall increase my stock of eggs. The others will lay. Before long, I shall have a chicken farm of quite substantial size. I shall be rich! And the young men will beg for my hand in marriage. I shall choose the strongest, the handsomest, and the richest, of course. And how my friends will envy me! I may even go to the city and buy myself a dress in the latest fashion for my wedding. It will be silk, and I shall have a new bonnet to match it. Everyone will say that I am the most elegant bride in the entire country!"

With this vain thought she tossed her head just as if she were already wearing her fine clothes. The milk can toppled from her head and the milk spilled all over the road. And the Maid had nothing to sell at the market that day.

Don't count your chickens before they are hatched.

From *Aesop's Fables*, edited by Elizabeth Stones

The Wind and the Sun

By Aesop

THE WIND and the Sun were disputing which was the stronger. Suddenly they saw a traveler coming down the road, and the Sun said,

"I see a way to decide our dispute. Whichever of us can cause that traveler to take off his cloak shall be regarded as the stronger. You begin."

So the Sun retired behind a cloud, and the Wind began to blow as hard as he could upon the traveler. But the harder he blew, the more closely did the traveler wrap his cloak round him, till at last the Wind had to give up in despair.

Then the Sun came out and shone in all his glory upon the traveler, who soon found it too hot to walk with his cloak on.

Kindness effects more than severity.

The Hare and the Tortoise

By Aesop

THE HARE was once boasting of his speed before the other animals. "I have never yet been beaten," said he, "when I put forth my full speed. I challenge anyone here to race with me."

The Tortoise said quietly, "I accept your challenge."

"That is a good joke," said the Hare. "I could dance round you all the way."

"Keep your boasting till you've beaten," answered the Tortoise. "Shall we race?"

So a course was fixed and a start was made. The Hare darted almost out of sight at once, but soon stopped and, to show his contempt for the Tortoise, lay down to have a nap.

The Tortoise plodded on and plodded on, and when the Hare awoke from his nap, he saw the Tortoise nearing the winning post, and could not run up in time to save the race. Then said the Tortoise,

"Plodding wins the race."

The Goose That Laid the Golden Egg

By Aesop

THERE was a Man who owned a Goose that laid a golden egg every morning. By selling these precious eggs, the Man was able to accumulate a store of wealth.

But the richer he grew, the greedier he became. He began to be dissatisfied with only one egg a day.

"Why not two eggs?" he thought, "or five or six? As a matter of fact, if I cut that bird open, I shall probably find a hundred eggs, and then I can retire and live in luxury for life!"

So thinking, he killed his Goose, cut her open, and, of course, found nothing.

He who wants more, often loses all.

From *Aesop's Fables*, edited by Elizabeth Stones